MOST VALUABLE PLAYER

MOST VALUABLE PLAYER

Peter Giant Bowleg

Library of Congress Control Number: 2020911447
ISBN: Hardcover 978-1-9845-8456-4
Softcover 978-1-9845-8455-7
eBook 978-1-9845-8454-0

This is a work of fiction. Names, characters, places and incidents either are the product of the author's imagination or are used fictitiously, and any resemblance to any actual persons, living or dead, events, or locales is entirely coincidental.

Print information available on the last page.

Rev. date: 06/19/2020

To order additional copies of this book, contact:
Xlibris
1-888-795-4274
www.Xlibris.com
Orders@Xlibris.com
815350

(I See GREATNESS In YOU...)

"...In order to Succeed...
You have to uncover the GREATNESS
Within... and.....**Take Flight**..."

"...Hidden inside anyone can be a Champion
waiting for the opportunity to shine
and become... **The MVP**..."

Peter Giant Bowleg

"...Most Valuable Player..."

(I See GREATNESS In YOU...)

"...Make your haters your Motivators...
Never Give IN, Never Ever Give UP...
The BEST Revenge is to LIVE the GOOD LIFE..."

-Julian "JB" Baxter – NBA Star
The Mystery Dunker

A Special Thank You to My "True Friends"...
A Very Special Thank you to ALL the
POSITIVE People that I have met...

Thank you for the Inspiration...
Thank you for the encouragement...

(I See GREATNESS In YOU...)

"...He who has a WHY to Live
Can bear almost any HOW..."
- Nietzsche

There comes a time in Life when You have to Draw a line in the sand...

Then...STAND...Your ground...
- Black Eagle/Peter Giant Bowleg

"...That which does not kill us...
Makes US STRONGER..."
- Nietzsche

...Believe...

ALL Things are POSSIBLE…

"...Most Valuable Player..."

(I See GREATNESS In YOU...)

This book is dedicated to my Mother – Theresa Fairweather and my brothers and sisters – Andrew, Judith, BJ, Ethan, Paulette, Stephanie, Trevor and John Jr along with their families. Thank you for your support...

A very special dedication to my two sons – Valentino and Tavares and their families.

Love to one and all...

Peter Giant Bowleg
writer/dreamer...

"...LISTEN...ENCOURAGE...INSPIRE...UPLIFT..."

Black Eagle Group Publishing...

"...LISTEN...ENCOURAGE...INSPIRE...UPLIFT..."

(I See GREATNESS In YOU...)

Acknowledgement

This book would not be possible if it were not for the Love, Inspiration, Encouragement, Sacrifices, Prayers and Support of a BLESSED, Wonderful, Loving and Powerful Lady by the name of Theresa Fairweather – My Mother. Through all the good times, bad times and in-between times mother always had a "word of encouragement" not only for her seven children but for everyone she knew or came in contact with. My mother was and always will be a "generous and caring person with her time, money and prayers". Thank you "Sexy Pepsi as she is known to the family". I truly appreciate you and the many sacrifices you have made for all of your children. I Love You Forever...

This book is also a "Thank You" to my brothers and sisters; Judy, Andrew, Ethan, Paulette, Trevor and BJ along with my sons Tavares and Valentino and their families. A special "Thank You" to my late grandparents; Romalia and George Albury of Nassau, Bahamas and my uncle Rick Albury of Harbour Island Bahamas. They watched over me and made sure I kept "on the right path" no matter the situation. Thank you to Miss Heidi Helm of Maximum One Realty, Mrs. Anita Bratton and Mr. Bratton, Catherine Yingling, Kelly, Brandi, Sabrina Fleming, Mrs. Ena Moncada, Debbie Hampton, Darlene Haffaney, Naja Finch and Scott Mmobuosi. A VERY Special "Thank You" to Franklin, Clarice Burr, Dominque Luna, Alexandria "Alex" Farmer, Khaadijah Wanja (Evangelist), Terry Bryant, Tigist "TG" Alemayehu, Jackie Auma, Mrs. Shayla Levy, Mrs. Robin Ellis, GG, Kathy Curtis, Mr. Cheatham, James, Sarah, Tyanne, Heaven, Gloria, Chiquita, Aziz, Carlo, Lucy, Caleb, Tyrone, Omar, Trent Goode, Lynasia Rhym, Erica Edwards, Jackie D, Torry Broom and Vernon Jones for being GREAT FRIENDS AND SUPPORTERS. An

"...Most Valuable Player..."

(I See GREATNESS In YOU...)

Extra Special Thank You to the team at the Publishing Company. Thank you to ALL the people that have made this book possible that I may have overlooked in naming them – Thank You one and ALL.

Be Blessed...

Peter Giant Bowleg
writer/dreamer...

"...LISTEN...ENCOURAGE...INSPIRE...UPLIFT..."

(I See GREATNESS In YOU...)

A very Special Thank You to the many strangers that stopped by The Locations and FedEx Office on Windy Hill as I was working on my books and writing... Thank you...

Thank you for all the encouragement, support and passion to get me to finish what I have started.

I am truly Blessed to have met each and every one of you... Especially Mrs. Bratton, Erica Edwards, Trent, Vernon Jones and My Baby Sis - Judith...

THANKS A Billion... Have an Amazing Day... May ALL Your Dreams Come True...

A Special Thank You to **"...The Mystery Lady..."**. Thank you for the INSPIRATION...

(I See GREATNESS In YOU...)

Thank You To The One That I "Love"...

A *Special Thank You* to the Lady that inspires me
to "Be the Best that I can be Each Day"...

Thank You for inspiring me to give my best
to everything I do each day...

You are the center of my world and I hope that you know and
believe that... Have an Amazing Day... Thinking of You...

Be Blessed...
May ALL your dreams, wishes and plans come true...

The Life Mantras of Julian
"The Mystery Dunker" Baxter

"...Make Your Haters Your Motivators...

"...The Best Revenge Is To Live The Good Life..."

"...Never Give In, Never Ever Give Up..."

(I See GREATNESS In YOU...)

Fiction:

This book - "Most Valuable Player (I See GREATNESS In You)" is "entirely fiction" and is not based on any story, book, person, TV series, another person's idea or movie. This book was created by Peter Giant Bowleg – alone. The story and characters were created as a direct result of the imagination of Peter Giant Bowleg. None of the characters are intended to resemble any living or dead persons. Any resemblance by name, description, or in any other way is strictly coincidental.

The book, the story, the characters were and are never intended to offend, insult, mistreat, deride, negatively impact, harass, humiliate or be derogatory, humiliating or condescending towards any person, group of people, association, organization or corporation. The book and characters that were created, named and originated are not intended to express hate, animosity, hard feelings or negativity towards any one, individual, person, organization, team or group. Any character resemblance to any person with a similar name, skills, look, athletic achievements, basketball player or professional living or dead is strictly coincidental. This book is "ENTIRELY FICTION".

"...Most Valuable Player..."

(I See GREATNESS In YOU...)

...Looking Back...

Julian Baxter felt as though he was going back in time as he recalled what had happened earlier in the day in Perimeter Mall. He had spotted a lady that had the same outline and walk as his high school crush; Samantha White. For some reason or another before he knew it; he had caught up with the lady and tapped her on the shoulder. She had spun around surprised by the touch and with a look of shock on her face. Shock that someone had out of the blue touched her person. She was about to give him the "riot response" but she recognized immediately that he was Julian "JB" Baxter star of the Atlanta Hawks basketball team and multi-millionaire. She had smiled and extended a hand. Julian Baxter was equally surprised because it was not Samantha White. He had shaken the young lady's hand and they had exchanged numbers and made small talk. The number that he had given her goes to the front office for the Atlanta Hawks Basketball team he did not have to worry about hearing from her again. However, he was a little disturbed that the memory of "the incident" that night and Samantha White stayed with him from so long ago. He had used "the incident" as a driving force. It had become a big chip on his shoulder and his heart. He used it to power his name and statistics up the rankings in Men's College Basketball and into the NBA as a first-round draft choice.

She had become his "energy drink" to power him up whenever he felt too tired to work out or he was having a rough game. He would think of her and "the incident" and then he would get an extra surge of energy and drive to score, play defense, rebound shots that were not even within his area. He became a madman whenever he thought of the "incident" with her. She probably only now (due to the internet and news stories) knows why he stopped calling, texting, writing and saying nothing beyond "Hi" to her. She probably did not find out until after he became the "Mystery Dunker" and the stories came out. Julian Baxter would never forget "the incident" as long as he lived.

Samantha White and her partner Ron Highland had not even seen Julian Baxter as he had watched from the shadows as the two of them had made out behind the gym on the back of Ron's car. Julian Baxter had had a crush on Samantha White from the beginning of middle school. He had finally built up the courage to speak with her after a whole lot of encouragement by his older brother, mother and father. He had spoken with her in the library foyer. A small "hi" had ended up with the two of them sitting on the steps of the library talking about everything. They had shared their hopes, dreams, likes and dislikes in a couple of hours. It was one of those rare times when she was alone and not surrounded by her usual entourage of other girls who tried to dress like her, act like her, walk like her, talk like her or want to be her. For some reason the two of them had connected as he had long hoped that they would. After talking for what seemed an eternity; they had visited the Library snack machines and then agreed to study together. As they sat side by side Julian Baxter felt as though he had died and gone to heaven.

The two of them had studied late that Friday night. They had missed their bus time. Julian called his mother and asked her to pick him and Samantha White up at the school library. His mother had said to him on the phone "THEE Samantha White" that you were always talking about. The Samantha White on the cheerleading squad? Julian had calmly told his mother "yes Mom" she needs a ride home. His mother had dropped everything at the house and raced to the library to pick them up. She had always told Julian and his brother Randall that they could be, do or achieve anything they set their minds to do. She and her husband had encouraged Julian to speak with Samantha and give it his best shot instead of "pining away over her and not making an effort to speak with her".

"...Most Valuable Player..."

Mrs. Angela Baxter had picked up Samantha and Julian as quickly as she could. She had offered to take them for ice cream; but Samantha had declined stating she had already overstayed at the library. Mrs. Baxter drove her home and made sure that she got inside. Julian had walked her to the door and Samantha had asked him to call her when he got home. They shook hands and said good night. Julian waited until Samantha had closed the door to her home and floated/raced to his Mother's car. Mrs. Baxter loved seeing her son so happy now that he had finally spoken with "the crush of his young life". His mother drove away from Samantha's home. A short distance away Mrs. Baxter pulled into a small strip mall parking lot to speak with Julian. She told Julian to take things slowly with Samantha. Talk with her about her day, her clothes, her dreams, her desires. Speak only of yourself if she asks you a direct question. Do not be too aggressive or expect too much right-away. Remember always, "You are not married to her and she is not married to you".

People will speak with Samantha when you are around respect that. Mrs. Baxter also cautioned Julian to not take it for granted that the way you feel about someone means that they feel as strongly about you. If the relationship fades out remember that there are other fish in the sea. Julian was listening to his Mom; but he was only listening partially. He was on top of the world. He had finally spent time with the lady of his dreams. He was on cloud 9,999,999,999.

His Mom hi-fived Julian when they got out of the car at home and headed into the house. She took her time and reminded Julian that he had to make a phone call. He quickly raced to his room to call Samantha White. They picked up right where they had left off at the library. Mrs. Angela Baxter was very happy for Julian, but she did not want him to get too high over the relationship in case things went sideways. Samantha and Julian were a couple until they hit the end of their sophomore year in High School.

"...Most Valuable Player..."

In high school freshman and sophomore year Julian was on the bench for the basketball team and he would watch as Samantha White became head cheerleader. She was also one of the most popular girls in the high school. She and Julian stayed true to each other. Samantha would go to basketball practices and watch Julian work with the team. He had a growth spurt and was nearing 6' 8" in High School but for some reason he was not on the starting five. She thought he was a good basketball player, but the coach kept him on the bench. Julian would play with his brother Randall Baxter in the nights and on the weekend to work on improving his game. Randall Baxter was a wide receiver on the football team at a top five High School football team.

Randall was considered one of the top 10 football players in the state of Georgia. He also was a better than decent basketball player. He would feed Julian the ball when he practiced his jump shots and free throws.

Their dad; Andrew Baxter had been a track star. He had run the 100 and 200-meters races. Their mother was the "true athlete in the family". She had starred in basketball in high school, college and the WNBA for a short time. Angela Baxter had torn up her knee and after recovering well enough to walk again she had called it quits from sports. She joined SunTrust Bank. She had quickly moved up the ranks. After college and some pro track and field time Andrew Baxter had begun to use his engineering degree from Georgia Tech and joined the Lockheed Martin Corporation. The two boys; Julian and Randall had inherited their parent's sports genes. While Randall had quickly blossomed and become a star in high school with the football team Julian could play basketball but was not the top scorer or the top rebounder. He played well in practice but in the games; he was not the same player. He was tall and still growing. He was strong when he rebounded the ball. He could ball handle better than most and had a smooth shot. He just did not play the same in games as in practice. The coaches spoke with him about it. His brother, his mother and his father, friends and teammates tried to help; no luck. Freshman and Sophomore years in High School while his brother starred across town Julian sat on the bench. Julian continued to play well during practice times, but he was not playing the same once the games became real. His coaches kept encouraging him and telling him that things would change one day. Julian kept wondering to himself "when things would change for him".

The brothers went to different schools because one had a strong basketball team and the other had a strong football team. The only consolation for Julian Baxter was he was going out with Samantha White. Julian and Samantha were inseparable.

Then "The Incident" happened and Julian Baxter's life was changed forever. He only told his brother Randall Baxter about it. He just stopped speaking with Samantha White or about her. He removed all of her photos, posters and cards from his room and put them in a box in the basement.

Julian took all the presents that she had given him and packed those in a box in the basement as well. Samantha for a while would call the house to speak with Julian but he would not answer or when he did; it was always to tell Samantha he had to practice. Julian would go to the court in the back of their house and practice and practice. Layups, Free throws, Jumpers, Trick shots, Long shots, basketball dribbling drills and he would practice dunk shots that he had seen on TV or on the DVD's. When Julian saw Samantha at school he was always late for class. When she called usually Julian would let it go to voice mail and then deleted them.

What had happened ("the incident") was the school had had an end of year dance at the new gym. The whole school had pretty much turned up. Julian got separated from Samantha. He had been talking with some classmates about their upcoming junior year, their college goals and dreams. After a while Julian noticed that Samantha White was no-where to be found. She had been beside him but had disappeared. Julian immediately began looking for her all over the building.

Julian looked for her all over the gym. He had gone to the second floor where a lot of people were occupying tables. Julian had even gone to the third-floor patio. One of the guys on the football team named Eric Moore had pulled Julian to the side. He told him to hurry up and find his girl as he had seen the quarterback for the football team; Ron Highland talking with her earlier. He said that guy is a backstabber. Julian told him thanks and went to the front of the gym where other people were gathered; no one had seen Samantha. He headed over to the main school building to see if the library was still open. He decided to take a shortcut by going behind the gym. And that was when he witnessed "the incident".

Julian thought he heard grunting and groaning. He moved towards the sound and the sight made him rub and scratch his eyes as if he was seeing things. The sight also made him question his sanity.

There was Ron Highland, quarterback of the school football team having sex with his girl; Samantha White. Samantha was on the back trunk of Ron's Camaro with her legs spread wide. Julian and Samantha had had sex more than a few times but not out in the open like this.

Julian was too stunned to move. He watched as if hypnotized as Ron pounded away at Samantha White and she pushed back just as hard from the trunk of the car. Finally, Ron came. He collapsed on top of Samantha. A Short time later he stood up and Samantha kneeled down to pull the condom off Ron. She tossed the used condom; then turned and gave Ron a long passionate kiss.

Samantha White and Ron Highland locked lips for the longest as Julian silently watched, and his heart shattered into a billion pieces. Julian's stomach turned as he watched the events unfold. Julian's eyes began to pour out tears. He wanted to move but was frozen in place. He could not even speak. How long had this been going on? Julian thought he would end up married to Samantha White. Julian watched as Ron got some hand towels from the trunk of his car and cleaned up. Samantha did the same. They sprayed body spray on each other and headed around to the front of the gym. Julian followed in the distance. He watched as they walked around to the front of the building arms around each other until they were near the front. They kissed again for a long time and then Samantha left Ron there to go back into the gym first. Ron gave her a quick pat on the ass as she walked away. Samantha White turned and smiled at Ron. Julian's first thoughts were to obliterate Ron from the face of the earth. He would not see him coming as he was already distracted watching Samantha walk away. Julian stayed in the shadows and watched as Ron walked to the front and then began talking with some other guys from the football team. Julian leaned against the building for a while tears streaming down his face.

Julian decided he did not want to face Samantha right now. It would not be a good scene. Julian did not want to see Ron either. He headed for the street and began walking home. It was a little over 20-mile hike. Julian did not want to take the bus. He just wanted to be alone. Julian knew that he needed to be alone right now. He headed to a nearby gas station and bought a big bottle of Smart Water, a large Kit Kat chocolate bar and a large can of Pepsi soda.

Julian did not say bye to anyone. It was vacation time and they would be coming back as Juniors in a few months. Julian began drinking the Pepsi and thinking why? What had he done that Samantha would betray him like this? Julian walked on as the tears began to fall like rain. His body began to shudder and shake. His breath caught as he first became angry and then resentful. Halfway home he had calmed down and was drinking only the water. His clothes were soaked through and through with sweat; but Julian did not care about appearances right now. He kept walking towards home. One step at a time. He thought deeply of what he had done or could have done to Samantha to cause her to cheat on him.

Finally, he reached home. He was totally soaked with sweat from head to toe as a result of the walk and his anger from what he had seen. Thankfully when he opened the door and walked in his Mom had already turned in. Julian went to his room and put on a pair of sweatpants, sneakers and a dry t-shirt. He went to his walls and took down all the photos of Samantha White. Julian took all the cards and gifts that Samantha had given him and put them in two garbage bags. He went to his brother's room and woke him up. He asked for his advice on something. He swore him to secrecy and told him not to ever tell anyone what he was about to tell him. He needed his advice. The tone in his younger brother's voice made Randall snap awake and sit straight up right away. He told Julian that he hoped that he had not been hanging out with the neighborhood gang guys. Julian told him "no it was nothing like that". He then told him what he had seen with Samantha White. Julian called it "The Incident".

After hearing the details of "the incident" Randall asked his baby brother Julian; what the hell are you going to do? Julian said that he was going to do nothing. What could he do? She was not married to him. Randall said remember you have to go to basketball camp in Florida this summer on vacation so you will be away from everyone. When you come back you will have to choose how to respond. Randall asked Julian what was he going to tell Mom and Dad as they really loved and adored Samantha White? Julian said he was going to tell them the truth in a way; she had moved on from him to someone else. Randall asked Julian if he did not want him to get some of his teammates to crush Ron? Julian said no things have a way of working out. Randall gave Julian a hug and told him that he was there for him. The brothers shook hands and said goodnight.

Julian could not sleep. In his room he turned on the TV and watched the news, the sports and then he turned to MSN by accident. He saw the stories of people who had overcome adversity and become millionaires and billionaires. He heard one man talking about how he was mistreated in high school and college. He had dropped out and become a multi-billionaire with a computer company he started. Some of the people that had teased him now applied to work at his companies and he said; "No Way". One of the successful men said he had a few mantras and sayings that kept him going all the time – "Make your haters your motivators". He said whenever he was tired or could not solve a problem; he recalled the incidents of the teasing and bad treatment that he had received in High School and College.

The Billionaire said he was then much more motivated to solve his problems and move forward. Julian smiled and made a note of the slogans and mantras "MAKE YOUR HATERS YOUR MOTIVATORS". "THE BEST REVENGE IS TO LIVE THE GOOD LIFE". "NEVER GIVE IN, NEVER EVER GIVE UP". He had been hurt to the core by what he had seen. He decided right then that he would use that vision as "fuel" to propel him to the rim for powerful dunks.

Julian had always treated Samantha White with love, respect, care, tenderness and was now totally heart-broken over what he had seen. It made him question everything about her. Now he was angry. Julian also realized that he had an outlet and a means to revenge. He would become the best basketball player that he could be. He would take out his revenge on every team they played. If he did not play in the games that mattered; then he would take things out on everyone in practice. He was going to get rid of his pain by making his opponents pay. He was going to the basketball camp and he would learn and learn and then learn some more. He would get better. He would work hard to become the best he could be and in that way; he would get his revenge. All his opponents would feel his pain. Julian knew his Mom was a basketball junkie and had always prodded him to be better. He would use that encouragement to his advantage. He made notes and then fired up his computer. He looked at the best of the past years in the NBA at various times. He saw Michael Jordan, Dr. J, Larry Bird, Magic Johnson, George "Iceman" Gervin, Shawn Kemp, Dominique, Lebron James, Curry, Kobe, Klay Thompson and others. He was going to study, learn and get better. They would be his instructors. He just had to get better at basketball.

Julian made a list of the tapes that he wanted along with a basketball shoe that helped a person to increase their vertical jump. Julian put the list on the table with his mother's name on it. Julian also needed two skipping ropes. He would carry one with him and leave the other at home. Every chance he got he would jump rope and stretch. He sat up watching the games of various individuals. He made notes of different things. He watched the And1 basketball series and saw the various stars do their thing. He knew he was going to get better. He watched tapes of Dennis Rodman, KG and Moses Malone rebounding. He began doing sit-ups, crunches and pushups. If his core was strong everything else would take care of itself. He would start with two sets of 50 crunches, sit-ups and pushups every morning and night.

Julian would make sure to stretch and take up Tai Chi and Yoga as he had heard that those two Programs would help him stay limber and loose. Julian began to study the moves of the best on and off the court. No more playing around. He was going to get serious about the game of basketball. Julian set his sights on becoming the best basketball player that he could be. He was about to become a star. He could feel it. He had just over two and a half weeks to the basketball camp. Julian knew he had to become a better defender on the basketball court. He figured the scoring part was easier to learn. Much harder to learn was taking on bigger and quicker players and defending them. He knew he would have to start there. He would also study how to block shots one on one and from behind. He would be a force to reckon with on both ends of the court. Julian decided he would get to practice early and talk with the coaches. He would seek advice on how to become a better defender and rebounder. He would talk to and work extra with the coaches at camp and when he came back from the camp.

He would get their assessment of what he needed to improve on and work hard at it. Julian figured if he became a better rebounder, ball handler and scorer the NBA was a possibility. He had a B+ average so being able to get into College was not an issue from a school grades perspective. Julian put the sayings "...The best revenge is to Live the Good Life...", "Make Your Haters Your Motivators" and "Never Give In, Never Ever Give Up" in all of his books and on a page of his phone to look at. They would keep him motivated. Julian did not know what his scoring, rebounding and assist stats were from the past year. He was starting anew from this point forward. What he did from this moment forward would matter. He made peace with the things in his life. He had fallen hard for Samantha White. Julian thought he and Samantha White had connected totally and she was his "Angel". He had treated her like a queen. She had gone behind his back and totally disrespected him. He had started to wonder if this relationship was going on for a while behind his back. Julian decided not to torture himself with thoughts of it. He had seen enough. She had hurt him to the core. It was time to go forward and focus on the future. He would begin running and practicing daily until it was time for camp.

Julian went to the garage area and found some lengths of light chain that belonged to his father. Julian selected a piece of chain that was long enough for him to skip with. He took the chain to his room and put it on the nightstand. It was 4:30am when he went to sleep. Julian set his alarm for 10am to wake up.

Samantha White was concerned. She had not heard from Julian. She had been unable to find him at the dance when she came back inside. No one knew where he was or where he had gone. Some students had told her that Julian was looking for her and then had disappeared. Here it was 3pm on Saturday after the dance and he had not called, emailed or texted her. Samantha White had called his cell number and it said; "not in service". Unknown to her Julian had changed his cell phone number and had only told his close friends and family about it. He told all of them not to give the info out to "anyone". Julian had also closed down all his social media accounts. No more Twitter, Snap chat, Facebook, google, Flickr or YouTube or any other accounts. He set up new Gmail and Yahoo accounts. He used "the Phoenix" symbol as his new calling card. Out of the ashes he would rise. Julian tossed and turned for a good while as the images of Samantha and Ron having sex replayed again and again in his mind. Finally, as dawn broke Julian went to sleep. He was so tired that he did not even hear the alarm clock. Since school was out for the break his Mother had let him sleep. Unbeknownst to Julian. Randall had told his mother (Mrs. Angela Baxter) what had happened. Randall stressed to his mother Angela that Julian had not done anything wrong to Samantha White and he had no intention of harming her. He had sworn me to secrecy and made me promise not to beat up Ron Highland. Randall however smiled when he made mention that next season his team plays Ron's team two times and he would ensure that there was a measure of "payback for his little brother". On learning of this and seeing the list on the table Angela Baxter had quickly run to the sports store and bought new sneakers, cross trainers, sweat suits, training gear, basketballs and three new jump ropes for Julian.

Mrs. Baxter ordered the videos and the special shoes that Julian had requested. Mrs. Angela Baxter put all of the items that she had purchased for Julian in his bedroom on the bureau and on the bed. He was sound asleep. Mrs. Baxter hoped that by Julian becoming more interested in basketball he would have an outlet for his anger and disappointment. She cooked Julian's favorite meal of baked chicken, potato salad, macaroni, peas and rice. She made fresh tossed salad for him and put the French dressing on the table. She put a Pepsi on the table and then went and banged on the door of Julian's room. "Wake up sleepy head" she called out. Mrs. Baxter heard groaning and stumbling around in Julian's room. She hollered it's already after 4pm. You need to eat so you can grow. That hit a button with Julian. He raced into the shower and then when he came out; he saw the new clothes and stuff. There were new basketball shorts, new sneakers, sweat bands, new t-shirts with motivational slogans on them. There were sweat suits and DVD's of NBA Greats, WNBA Greats as well as And1 games. There was lots of new sport underwear and socks (tons of it). Three new Basketballs. He put on a pair of shorts, cross trainer sneakers, training sweats and a hoodie. He saw the new jump ropes. Julian dressed quickly and raced to the dinner table. His Mom said grace and told him good luck with the training. She gave him a hug and kiss on the cheek and disappeared. Based on what Randall had told her she knew Julian was hurting but instead of being angry or crying he was channeling it into basketball. In a way, it was an answer to her prayers. Angela Baxter had played basketball all her life and saw untapped potential in her youngest child. She knew from experience that for some people it took a life-changing event for the basketball light bulb to go off.

Mrs. Baxter believed that this was what had happened to Julian. She hoped and prayed that she was right. She said a prayer and then went back to check on him. Mrs. Baxter knew that she would have to "play dumb" when it came to Samantha White. At some point she was going to have to let her husband know what happened to Julian.

Mrs. Baxter told her youngest son; Julian "anytime he was ready to learn how to shoot and really play basketball to let her know and she would lace up her sneakers and show him". Julian responded, "Aww Mom you don't have to rub it in". Then his confidence came out when he told her "wait until after basketball camp in three weeks and you won't be saying nothing but praise when I get back in town; you wait" he told her. His response had caught Angela Baxter totally off guard. He had never spoken this confidently before. He must now see what she had always seen in him "the potential for Julian to be a great basketball player". The Samantha White matter would resolve itself in time.

Julian ate up. Once he was full, he washed the dishes and put them away. He saw that his mom had bought his favorite flavor ice cream – chocolate. He got a dish full and headed to his room to watch the DVD's. Julian saw that five new notebooks were on his computer station along with new DVD's from And1 and others. He could only think of one person who did it; his Mom (Angela Baxter). His father was away on a Lockheed Martin top secret project for another three months. He said a silent "Thank you" and began to watch the DVD's and learn. He watched the dribbling, the take off's, the shooting and the blocking attempts. He had to learn that George Gervin flip. He had to learn to cup the ball the way that Dr. J and Shawn Kemp did it. Julian made notes of the various moves and issues.

Julian also had to learn to use the finger roll to drive defenders crazy. Gervin would flip the ball just high enough that no matter who jumped to block his shot it always was too high for them. Julian soaked it all in. He recalled how at times in practice he would be hitting shots from everywhere and then he could not hit "the ocean" if it was a basket. He would figure it out. All it would take is time, studying the game and lots of practice. Julian promised himself that he would go-all out to get better at the game of basketball.

Julian watched a special on sports greats and there was a national commentator that said the difference between the best and the average is "the mentality". The best believe that they are and go out and show it every game. The average players do not have that belief and confidence. Doubts creep in if they miss two shots in a row or if they get their shot blocked. The Larry Birds, Magic Johnsons, Michael Jordan's and others keep shooting. Eventually the misses will start going in for points. But if you do not keep shooting after misses the percentage never goes up. Julian remembered the times when he stopped shooting. That will not happen in the future. He was going to get better. If the outside shots are not falling; he would drive or pass to others. Julian studied and studied. Then he got some rest until the sun dipped a bit and then he would work on his free throws and dribbling. He also would begin his skipping regimen. He gazed at his new belongings. His mother had bought him a new gym bag. It was a new day and a new Julian Baxter. He felt refreshed and reborn. Julian stretched out on his bed to rest. He reflected on the lessons he had learned from the video tapes and ESPN Specials.

Julian woke up a few hours later. He grabbed one of the new skipping ropes and headed to the garage. In the garage; he grabbed one of the new basketballs and headed to the backyard basketball court. Julian put the Gatorade, towel and skipping rope on the bench his father had created.

Julian began with some light stretching and then slow jogs up and down the court. He stretched some more and then jumped rope for 15 minutes. Now it was show time. He ran a few lay ups and then he decided to take 30 free throws. He tried to make as many as he could. He was not trying to make a specific number; he was trying to formulate a rhythm for when he was taking a free throw. Julian kept shooting until he had shot 30 times.

Julian put the ball down and skipped for 15 minutes after a brief rest. Then he began to work on his footwork. He ran shuffle drills from one end of the court to the other. Julian remembered that coaches were always preaching "sit down" on that drill and shuffle the feet. The coaches always said keep the hands up. He sat for a while to review what he did right and what he needed to improve on. He completed drinking the first large Gatorade drink and started on the second one.

Julian started over. His cell phone rang. It was his brother Randall checking on him. He told his brother that he was doing much better. He was in the backyard on the court working on his "poor free throw shooting". Randall told Julian that he had to stop worrying about the score, the other team or anything when he was shooting free throws. Focus on the rim and believe that he would make all of them.

Randall told Julian to concentrate on his mechanics; release motion and follow through. Julian thanked his brother for the advice and support and promised to work on it. Later, Julian heard a car pull up in the driveway. He looked around the house to see Samantha White getting out of her car. Julian did not want to speak with her at all. Without hesitating; he was over the fence with his ball and skipping rope. He headed to a neighbor five houses down named Pablo Jones. Julian wanted to get there before Samantha White came out of the house and began looking for him. Knowing his mother Julian figured his Mom would check his room and then the basketball court. By then he should be safely at Pablo's house. They had played basketball together; but Pablo had decided to try out for the football team. Pablo had made the starting lineup on the football team as a cornerback. He was a hard worker. Pablo and Julian had remained close friends. Julian would go to his high school football games to cheer Pablo on. The team might not be great, but Pablo had made a name for himself. Pablo had put in the work and effort. He was now All State at Cornerback. Pablo was one of Julian's few constant supporters. When he was not playing or practicing football Pablo would come to Julian's basketball games and chant for Julian to be put in the game. When Pablo opened the front-door Julian told him he needed his help. He was working on his jump shots and free throws. Pablo waved him in; and they marched to the kitchen for more Gatorade and then onto the basketball court in the back of Pablo's home. Pablo told Julian he figured that he would be somewhere cuddled up with Samantha White. Julian told Pablo "straight up" that he and Samantha White were no longer dating or speaking.

Julian told Pablo that he was working on his game. He wanted to be a starter next year. Pablo and Julian shot free throws and jump shots for almost two hours. Pablo told Julian to keep working by next semester he would truly be a starter then on to a future in the NBA. They shook hands and Julian headed home. Julian was encouraged by the words of "his number one supporter outside of his family". He smiled as he was on his way to phase one of his goals. Phase one was to make his high school basketball team as a starter. Phase two was to get into College and Phase three was to make the NBA or one of the foreign leagues. Time would tell the true story of everything.

Julian had forgotten to do his pushups, sit-ups and crunches. He had also left his phone and other materials in his back yard. Julian had been in a hurry to avoid contact with Samantha White. He went around to the back of the house and saw that his towel, watch and phone were not there. He headed to his room. His towel, watch and phone were in his room. There was also a card from Samantha. Julian took the card from Samantha and tossed it unopened into one of the bags with other goods she had given him. He went to find his mother and told her that he had gone over to his friend Pablo's and had not paid attention.

Julian's mother knew the what and why he had gone and left his belongings in the back yard. She said nothing. She only told him that Samantha White came by looking for him and had left him a card. He told his Mom thanks and that he had found it. Julian began his pushups, then his crunches and sit-ups. The journey had begun.

Samantha White was upset. She had been dating Julian Baxter for close to two-years and now since the dance she had not heard a peep from him. His cell phone number was not working. He had probably changed his number. They usually talked about everything. He loved her; she knew that by the way he treated her and communicated with her.

Julian was also a smooth lover. They had made love several times and when he touched her, he moved her in so many ways. Now this; he was not even making an effort to contact her. Why? They were always constantly talking, texting or emailing each other. Had Julian found out that she had had sex with Ron Highland. Ron had been after her for a long, long while and she had "risked everything" and given him "a taste" last night at the dance. There was no one around. There were no witnesses. It was only the two of them. This was the one and only time she had been unfaithful to Julian. Had Julian found out about it or had Ron talked about it? If he had it would be his word against her word.

Samantha called Ron and asked if he had spoken with anyone about what happened at the dance? He told her no he had not and would not. Ron began to tell Samantha again as he had many, many, many times before that he wanted her to be his girl. He stressed to her why date a man that rides the bench. You can have me a "starter" and a true athlete.

Samantha had been seriously considering leaving Julian for Ron for a while but had decided to stay with Julian. Now Julian has gone missing. He had shut down his email accounts along with all his social media accounts.

For the first time in her young life Samantha White had no answers. She had not ever chased Julian before but this time she went to his house looking for him and he was not there. All of his classmates gave her the old phone number and email addresses that were not working. Mrs. Angela Baxter smiled as she saw the look on Samantha's face when they had found that Julian was nowhere around. Mrs. Baxter could have sworn Julian was working on his free throw shooting in the back yard but when they went out there, he was not there. Mrs. Baxter was betting that when Julian saw that the car which had pulled up in their driveway belonged to Samantha White he had taken off. Her best guess was that Julian was probably at Pablo's home five houses down the street; but she would never send Samantha there.

Whatever was going on Julian would speak to her when the time was right. At the moment, he was trying to find his way out of the fog. He had been fantasizing about Samantha White for a long, long, long time and he had finally gotten with her. Now it had gone sideways. Julian was trying to fight his way to the surface as he was in danger of drowning due to the hurt feelings and broken heart. His mother commended him. He was fighting back the only way he knew how.

Julian was showing that he was a lot tougher than she or her husband thought that he was. The fact that he had walked 20-plus miles home from the dance also spoke volumes about his determination.

Julian completed his regimen and caught a shower. He put on a fresh set of t-shirt, socks and underwear. Julian still had to shoot some more after dinner. He ate grilled fish, coleslaw, lots of broccoli, brown rice and baked potatoes. He had a Pepsi and then lots of cold water. His mother said nothing about Samantha White or his new practice in the back yard. She acted as if nothing was wrong. Mrs. Baxter figured in time Julian would come to her with questions about the game of basketball. If not, she was ok with that too. Prior to Andrew Baxter leaving for his work seminar trip he, Julian, Randall and Angela had talked about college dreams and plans. Julian and Randall both wanted to go to Florida schools. Julian wanted to go to the University of Florida and Randall wanted to go to Florida State. Randall had a good chance at a scholarship. He had the grades and football experience. Julian had the grades to go to University of Florida but to play basketball he would have to be a walk-on. That would mean paying for the first two semesters until he proved himself unless he improved his basketball this upcoming year and was able to get a scholarship. Andrew and Angela had some savings already in place for both boys to go to College at least the first two years. They would need to increase their input for the four years or draw down from their individual 401K plans to cover school fees for both boys. If they both drew down from their 401K's and got an education loan they would be ok.

They also had equity in their home to draw down on. Andrew Baxter did not care what they had to do. If the boys did not get full-ride-sport scholarships; they were still both going to College. He was adamant about that. Even if it meant they only got undergraduate degrees. If Randall had another good year with his high school football team; he would be four-star rated. Randall would have three years starting under his belt and schools would want to look closer at him. He could possibly get a scholarship offer or two. If Randall received a football scholarship that would give them the additional money to fund college for Julian.

Andrew and Angela agreed to contact their respective HR Manager and the Departments to see what funds were available to be withdrawn from their 401K's in a year. It was long ago agreed to that Randall would go to Football camp and Julian would go to Basketball camp. Each would be gone for almost the entire summer vacation. The camps were already paid for and money saved for extras for the two boys. Angela got up early Sunday morning to go to Church at Mount Paran Church of God on Cobb Parkway near I75 south. After Church she headed to Dick's Sporting goods store to get extra sweat suits, t-shirts, shorts, gloves, sneakers, cleats, underwear and socks for Randall to wear at his camp. When Mrs. Baxter returned home, she placed Randall's packages and new gym bag in his room. She cooked baked chicken, peas and rice, potato salad, coleslaw, mash potato and brought chocolate and strawberry ice cream for dessert. Mrs. Baxter had to bring home a triple dose of straw berry ice cream as her son Randall also liked strawberry ice cream. It was always a dog fight between the two of them.

Randall and his Mom went to the living room to play video games after eating. Julian headed to his room to stretch and then complete his required 50 crunches, sit-ups and push-ups. He stretched some more and took a shower. He put on his PJ's and began watching tapes of Vince Carter and his amazing vertical. He also watched tapes of Michael Jordan and how he dissected various teams. Jordan was the same size as Julian. Julian began to laugh. He had hops. He only needed to work on the other parts of his game and bring it all together. He was going to punish people. Julian could see his future in basketball. He had a premonition. He smiled and jumped into bed.

While Julian was happily falling asleep; on the other side of town Samantha White was fuming and upset. She had not heard from Julian Baxter. It was almost as if he "had dropped off the face of the earth".

Her friends had told her that at the dance on Friday night Julian was rushing to and fro asking everyone had they seen her. He had been trying non-stop to find her. Then Julian had disappeared. He had simply vanished after most people had seen him looking for her. Everyone asked Samantha White where she was; and she had never fully answered that question. All her schoolmates, friends and classmates had checked Julian's social media pages. Julian's social media pages (Facebook, Instagram, Twitter and others) had been wiped clean and shut down. No one knew how to email or phone him. His phone number had been disconnected. His email had been changed. He was not home when she called his home phone and spoke with his brother and mother.

Samantha concluded that he might have gone to visit other family members. Ron was continually blowing up her phone now that he had had a "taste" of her. If she did not hear from Julian soon, she might have to take Ron up on his offer to meet up at a hotel. Samantha White had not heard anything about her and Ron. He truly must be able to keep a secret.

Right then Samantha's phone lit up with an email from Ron saying he was thinking of her and wondered what she was doing Monday night? He lived in Decatur and she lived in Marietta. He wanted them to meet at the Hilton Hotel near Midtown. It was on the edge of downtown and easy to get into and out of. Ron said he would pay for valet parking and the room. They could spend the night if they wanted to. Samantha White called her friend Rachel Sanchez and told her that if anyone contacted her; she was spending the night there Monday. Rachel said she did not want to know what was going on. She told Samantha that she hoped she was not "stepping out on Julian". Julian is a good man with a bright future; and you may be blowing it all due to your huge ego if you have not done so already Rachel told Samantha.

Everyone from school have called me and emailed me since Friday night saying how come Julian is not on Facebook or any social media since then? He seemed to have shut down his phone number, email accounts and social media between Friday night/Saturday morning. Rachel said she had seen Julian at the dance when he was looking for her. Rachel and Pablo had been contacted by Julian and given his new number. They were told not to give the number to anyone.

Rachel told Samantha that it was "extremely painful and heartbreaking" to watch Julian go from group to group and table to table looking for you and be unable to find you. Rachel reminded Samantha White that Julian had done everything he could to treat her like a queen. Samantha for a moment had second thoughts about meeting up with Ron but she told Rachel that things were under control. She told Rachel that if anyone called, she was staying with her over-night but she was out at the moment. Rachel pleaded with Samantha to tell Julian it was over if she was planning to meet up with someone else. At least give him that amount of respect. He has been crazy about you for a long, long, long time. Everyone in school knows it.

No one was happier for him than me when he hooked up with you. He was always talking about you. He would look at you and it was like he was seeing you for the first time each time he saw you. You make a perfect couple. Samantha said; "something had come up".

Rachel told her to go and do her thing but one day she may regret it; really regret how she has treated Julian. Rachel hung up. She wanted to curse out Samantha so badly. Rachel figured Samantha was cheating on Julian and all he had done was treat her like a queen. He had never hit her. He had never abused her love. He had never complained even when she flirted with other guys at games and events when he was around. Rachel said out loud that it was women like Samantha White that caused good men to hate Black women.

Rachel felt she would never forget the pained look on Julian's face as he raced from table to table and group to group looking for Samantha at the dance. Rachel said a silent prayer that Julian would come out of the relationship with Samantha White stronger and better off than when he went into it.

Early Monday morning Angela Baxter called her husband Andrew to let him know that Julian and Samantha were no longer a couple. Something happened, and Julian is not talking but he climbed over the back fence today and left. Samantha came to visit, and he saw that it was her car in the driveway. He left without speaking with her. He left his phone, watch and other materials in the back yard. Andrew asked his wife if she had confronted him about his reason for running away when he saw her car pull up? She said no she was giving him his space right now. He has taken an intense new-found interest in basketball now. He is also still growing. He is 6' 8" now and should reach 6' 10" to 6' 11" and if he works a little bit harder; he can have a future in the sport. Andrew told his wife that he would follow her lead and do what she felt was best for him.

Andrew Baxter said he liked Samantha for Julian. Angela Baxter said she felt the same too, but something happened at the dance Friday night. Since then he has taken down all her photos, cards and stuffed animals she had given him and placed them in the basement. He has been working extremely hard at his basketball game and getting in shape. He also requested some DVD's and basketball equipment. I already ordered them for him.

Julian can ball handle. I watched him working in the back yard. He also has hops. I did not know he had a vertical like he showed today. I even saw him try a 360 dunk. He missed the three times that he tried it, but he was close. Mrs. Baxter told her husband Andrew; with the equipment that we have ordered his vertical should go up another two feet and he would easily make the 360 by the end of the summer vacation. By the way, he can two hand tomahawk dunk straight to the floor with a running start. He does it just like your favorite basketball player; Shawn Kemp of the Seattle Supersonics used to do. You know the one where he would put it behind his head with two hands and viciously power it through the hoop.

Mrs. Baxter told her husband that their baby son Julian even does that "spread leg thing" that Shawn Kemp, Michael Jordan, Kobe and Vince Carter would do. He's a quick learner. Andrew Baxter told his wife Angela that he would do whatever she said. He told her to do what was in the best interest of the family. It does not matter that they liked Samantha. He wanted his son to be happy. Andrew told Angela that there must be some good reason why Julian does not want anything to do with her. He told her that whenever Samantha shows up at the house from now on tell her Julian is not there. That one I am putting my foot down on. Angela agreed to do as he instructed. He said even if Julian walked into the house seconds before she pulls up; he is not available. Angela agreed to abide by her husband's wishes. Andrew told Angela that he loved her and missed her. She said the same to him and they both hung up.

Angela Baxter wanted to tell her husband what Randall had told her happened at the dance but decided that now was not the time to do so. She would tell him face-to-face. She would; however, follow his instructions and tell Samantha White that Julian was not available or home whenever she called or came by.

Randall passed by his mother on the way to the kitchen. Randall told his mother; "This Samantha White thing might be the best thing to happen to Julian in a reverse kind of way. Revenge is a powerful drug and it will power Julian to heights he never dreamed of before. He is young and taller than me and Dad. He is also still growing. If he becomes intense then the world is at his feet and no matter where he plays the NBA will come calling". Randall told his Mom; "Julian is going to be alright. Don't worry. He is about to become superman". Randall told his mom that he just has "a feeling about Julian". He hoped that he was right on target.

Randall said he watched from his bedroom window and saw Julian attacking the rim in the back yard and if he does that once in a game; Colleges will come calling to bring that out in him consistently. Randall said he was skipping breakfast. He and several members of his football team were meeting up to work out before the upcoming football camp. He had his thermos and all he needed was coffee. Randall gave his mother a hug and quickly filled his thermos with coffee and was out the door.

A short time later Mrs. Baxter heard the alarm go off in Julian's room. He started moving around in the room.

She knocked on the door and told Julian to have a great day she was off to work. Julian hollered back have a great day Mom and Love Ya. He resumed working on his two sets of 50 sit-ups, 50 pushups and 50 crunches. He would stretch again after working out and then catch a shower. Next, he had to fill up. His Mom had probably left him breakfast and all he had to do was heat it up. Yes, she had! His Mom had prepared his favorites. Julian had his own stack of hotcakes, sausages and scrambled eggs. While it warmed up in the microwave Julian made a cup of tea. He ate slowly. Then he looked at a couple of DVD's and internet sites on ball handling techniques.

Julian studied the top guards of the game; Chris Paul, Kyrie Irving, Walt "Clyde" Frazier, Steff Curry and others. He watched the past greats and especially Magic Johnson. Soon it was off to the backyard to work on his game. He had to get a better handle with his right hand. He was a lefty. He began dribbling the ball with his right hand with his left hand behind his back. Julian was gradually getting better. By the time the summer vacation was over he would be ready. He could feel it. He was planning to punish people with his game.

Julian worked on his crossover dribbles from each side. He worked on his between the leg and behind the back dribbling. Then he ran shuttle drills to improve his defense. He had to remember to sit down and slide. He began his layup drills. He attacked the rim as though the rim was Samantha and Ron and he was smacking them down. Julian was not paying attention to how high he was getting above the rim. He was just intent on making every dunk attempt.

Next Julian worked on his free throw shooting. He shot 30 attempts. He tried to follow the same motion each time. Then Julian worked on his jump shots off the dribble. He took a break for 20 minutes and then he started jumping rope again. It was 30 more free throws and then back to dribbling from one length of the court to the other with the right hand and then with the left hand and then switching hands and mixing in between the leg and behind the back dribbles. After his workout; Julian caught a shower and put on fresh clothing.

Julian caught a nap and then woke up to watch more game tape of Magic Johnson, Larry Bird, Dr. J, Shawn Kemp, Lebron James, MJ, Bernard King, Reggie Miller, Kobe and others. He made notes of things that he wanted to concentrate on. He worked to expand his vision on his layup drills. After resting he would jump rope for 10 to 15 minutes more and then stretch.

During his rest periods Julian would remind himself of things to concentrate on. He had to be on balance during his lay ups. Opposite hand from the take-off foot or he would be off balance and susceptible to coming down wrong or getting hurt. The objective was to hurt other people with his cross over dribbles, his blocked shots and his dunks. He worked on perfecting the two-handed power dunk that he saw Shawn Kemp throw down a lot. He also worked hard on the Vince Carter and MJ side-ways dunk that that made them look like they were flying. Julian figured the old adage of "if at first you don't succeed then keep on trying until you get it right" would work for him. He put in the time, energy and review of his actions. He believed if he put in enough practice time and dedication; the game would reward him in the end.

After several practice attempts Julian began to make the 180 with ease. The 360 dunk on-the-other hand was giving him fits. He was making the rotations but missing the dunk. He kept hitting the front of the rim. Once he improved his vertical it would come; he told himself. Julian made a note in his notebook to check with his Mom on the shoes he had requested to help improve his vertical. She said she had requested express shipment for the order. It should be to their home by Wednesday he figured. That would give him a week and a half to get used to them. Julian figured between the shoes and skipping rope he should soon get to a 44/52 inch vertical. With that vertical Julian would own the basketball courts and anyone that dared to guard him. He wanted a new number.

Julian would ask his coach about changing his jersey number to 13. It was going to be his lucky number and it was going to be unlucky for anyone that he would go up against. Julian texted his coach right away and had to make him aware that this was his new phone number. He told his coach that yes; he had not played much this past season but now he had set much higher expectations for himself.

Julian asked the coach if he could have the number that no one wanted; 13 as his number next year if he made the team? The number 13 was considered bad luck by most basketball players. Not this one! Julian's High School Coach, Gregg Randle told him he could definitely have the number 13 if he made the team. Julian told the coach prepare to meet a new man and new basketball player come the start of school and tryouts. Julian would be entering his Junior season in his high school.

Julian hung up and started laughing. He raced to his room and got out some poster boards and traced out the image of a basketball jersey with the number 13 in the front on one board and the back of the jersey on another board with his name. He was going to be starting at one forward slot and wearing the number 13. He used duct tape to attach the drawings of the new jersey to his bedroom walls. Julian wrote it on multiple sheets of paper and stuck it up all over the room and even in the bathroom. He set up a note page on his phone with his new number. JB Baxter - #13.

It was time to rest. Julian made sure that he had drunk plenty of water and Gatorade. He felt deep within that he had changed in some way. He did not know exactly what and why it was; but Julian felt different. He pulled the covers over himself after setting the alarm for 5:30pm. Julian made a note to get his Mom to bring him some power shakes, vitamins, supplements and protein shakes. He was out like a light. With no disturbances and interruptions Julian was getting his act together. He was now becoming a true basketball player. The drills were helping with his footwork. The skipping rope was helping with his vertical. When it all came together; he was going to be a "dynamic" force to reckon with. Julian also still had more growing to do. He was nearing 6' 9" tall and could top out at 6' 11" or 7' tall. He had a lot more work to do before Colleges would come calling but he now felt that he had the potential to make it. As Julian continued to practice; the free throws and the jump shots were beginning to fall with regularity. The constant practice, the videos, the studying of the game and various players were all having a Positive Impact.

Julian had been shooting a flat shot before. He changed to a higher arching shot like the top shooters he saw; Larry Bird, MJ, Reggie Miller, Klay Thompson, Lebron, Steff, Kobe and others. Saturday to Tuesday he could already feel the improvement. His mother had checked the order for the basketball equipment designed to improve the vertical of players and it was due Wednesday morning. She contacted the company herself. Julian went to sleep Tuesday extra excited about his game and having the ability to get higher above the rim easily appealed to him.

Shortly after 2pm Wednesday there was a knock on the front door and the mail man stated he had a package that had to be signed for. Julian retrieved his ID; showed it to the mailman and quickly signed for the package. It was his equipment and a video to go with it. He collected the other mail from the mail man. He closed and locked the front door. Julian raced to his room and opened the package. He saw the strange shoes that kept you on your toes all the time. He prayed that the device helped him. Julian looked at the video and saw the improvements of past clients. Julian was excited. He watched the video from the equipment maker two more times before taking them to the court to try them out. After strapping them on Julian felt like he was wearing high heeled shoes.

But he felt it had worked in helping others to improve their vertical jump and it would help him. Julian began working out in them. Soon "the strangeness" gave way to comfort. He worked out in them and then he stretched some more. Every day he trained; rain or shine.

In the rain he worked on the shuttle drills and footwork. When it was not raining Julian also worked on his free throw shooting, mid-range and long-distance shooting.

Julian constantly worked on his dribbling and even took over part of the garage when it was raining to practice. Two days before heading to basketball camp in Orlando, Florida it happened. Julian hit all his attempts at a 360 dunk. The world was now his. He would cup the ball in his left hand and spin clock-wise and dunk 360. He would cup the ball in his right hand and spin counter clock-wise and dunk 360. His mother watched from the window with pride but said nothing. His brother was also watching from his window and just let out a quiet yell. Randall thought to himself as he watched Julian take flight for one of his now patented Shawn Kemp power dunks; Samantha White had brought out the beast in his little brother.

Julian left for basketball camp in Orlando, Florida and Randall left town for North Carolina and football camp there. Mrs. Baxter took the quiet time in the home to call her husband and tell him what Randall had told him. Andrew Baxter got hotter than a raging fire. He became "totally speechless". Mrs. Baxter thought her husband was having a stroke and she constantly asked Andrew if he was ok. He finally found his voice and said; "that girl is a HO"...!!!! Mrs. Baxter laughed at her husband and said to him "that was wrong". Mrs. Baxter told her husband that he was wrong for calling Samantha White "a HO". Mr. Baxter emphatically defended his choice of words. He began to totally curse out Samantha White. He stated that he did not want Samantha White anywhere near his house, family and especially not near Julian.

Mrs. Baxter said Samantha might have found someone else and did not know how to tell Julian. "Whatever" said Mr. Baxter. Samantha White is no longer welcome in our home. Call the Police on her for trespassing if she comes there. Mrs. Baxter kept on laughing as her husband cursed, ranted and raved about Samantha White. Finally, Mr. Baxter calmed down. Mrs. Baxter said Samantha has not been by the house in three days. She thinks Julian is away. He truly is away now.

When Julian comes back from camp she is still not welcome in my house, my yard, my drive-way or in front of my home said Mr. Baxter. Mrs. Baxter told her husband Andrew that she was now sorry that she told him what Randall had been told by Julian. Julian calls it "the incident". Randall said he has not spoken to him about it since he came home that Friday night. He walked straight home from the school dance. Mr. Baxter asked his wife wasn't that gym dance almost 20-something miles away? Mrs. Baxter said yes; Julian came straight home on foot. He headed home right after witnessing Samantha and some guy named Ron from the football team making out behind the main hall. No one saw him. Julian has not spoken with anyone from school since except Pablo up the street. Mrs. Baxter said she believed Julian ran over there the day that Samantha White came by the house. Julian has changed his cell phone number and his email addresses.

He has also taken down all photos and posters of Samantha White. He put all the posters, photos, cards, letters and presents in two boxes in the basement and covered them up. Good for him said Mr. Baxter. Mrs. Baxter said there is some "good news" to tell you.

She told Mr. Baxter that if Julian clicks at the Florida basketball camp the way she has seen him play on the court practicing in the backyard he will certainly get scholarship offers. Due to the advanced classes he has been taking in school after this year he can go straight to College. He has extra credits already. I expect he will be in the starting five this year in high school and eventually in College somewhere. "Really...?" was all Mr. Baxter could say. He asked his wife if she was talking about Randall their oldest son. Mrs. Baxter said; "no it was Julian their baby boy". Mr. Baxter cautioned his wife to not go and get ahead of herself because he was their son. She told Andrew Baxter that she had been extra critical of Julian and his basketball playing because he "IS" their son.

Mrs. Baxter told her husband Andrew that she had bought Julian various DVD's and he has been studying the best in the NBA and College. He has improved in almost three weeks. He is now dunking 360 going both ways. Mr. Baxter asked his wife again; "if she was talking about Randall"? She laughed and told Mr. Baxter that she was talking about their baby son Julian. He is nearly 6' 9" tall now and still has more growing to do. Remember Randall is your height 6" 5". Julian is clearly taller than him now and the gap is growing. Since "the incident" Julian has been working out twice a day rain or shine. He is also watching videos and taking notes in his room. He has even changed the way he walks. He has a longer and easy stride now. The pushups and training he has been doing have given Julian a bolder and smoother walk. It's a confidence thing.

Mrs. Baxter told her husband that if Julian keeps improving as he has done to this point; the sky is the limit for him.

Mr. Baxter said we might not have to touch our 401K accounts if what you are saying is true. We will see what happens after the camp and school starts. Mr. Baxter told Mrs. Baxter to keep Samantha White away from Julian until he finds his bearings. She agreed. They exchanged "I Love You's" and each hung up. Mrs. Baxter could not stop laughing at how upset her husband had become over "the incident". She had never heard her husband cuss and call someone a "HO" before. She smiled. She sent an email to both boys letting them know their dad said "Hi".

Julian could not wait to get to basketball camp. At the airport he met other people also headed to the camp. Once their flight landed and they got to the baggage section there were members of the camp staff with lists of attendees. They helped the kids and their parents or chaperones get on the busses to the camp. For the most part Julian kept quiet and listened to the others talk about their dreams, goals and stats from last year.

Most of them talked as if they were starters on their teams. Julian rubbed his hands together and smiled. They would become his first victims. They would be the first to feel his pain. He paid attention as they talked about their games and what they needed to improve on. There was a welcome ceremony and various coaches were introduced. Julian took note of the names for the rebounding and shooting coaches. He walked up to each man after the opening ceremonies and gave them his name and information. Julian told them he wanted to improve and needed all the help that he could get. Both men agreed to give him time at lunch time and after sessions were over.

A couple attendees had not shown up at camp. Julian was one of the select few that received a room of his own. No roommate to disturb his workout regimens or ask inquisitive questions. After being assigned a room and unpacking. Julian decided to "explore the camp". There was a female basketball players camp and a male basketball players camp going on. The males and female camp attendees were kept apart. The area had two large gyms. The males used one and the ladies used the other. The layouts were the same for both gyms. There was one main court and other smaller courts around it as well as rims and free throw areas on the sides of the gyms so that many players could practice at the same time. The two gyms had spacious and fully stocked weight rooms. There were also two large pool areas. Julian and Randall had both been taught to swim by their parents. Their parents did not want them to be afraid or paranoid around water. Also, in case they fell in they would be able to survive. As Julian walked from the pool and cafeteria areas back to his room; he thought that swimming might be a great workout tool for him. He could build up his strength and stamina without the stress and pounding of running. Julian clapped his hands together and let out a shout of glee. "Ooooohhhh Yeahhhhhhhhhhh" Julian shouted. One more tool to help him get better. They also had a large number of sauna and whirlpool locations near the housing facility and spread out across the properties. Julian received a schedule of the activities. There was a welcome dinner and introduction session for later that night. The actual training camp would start early the next day. They would work out, rest, have meetings, watch tape and workout some more.

Near the end of the second week they would start scrimmages during their workouts. At the end of camp; the top 24 male and female players would be named to an All-Star Team. The two male teams would face off against each other with the males and females on hand. There would also be a dunk contest. Then the men's All-Star game would be held. An MVP would be chosen from the game.

Julian set no goals to win any awards. He just wanted to get better on defense, shooting and rebounding. He had found an internet site where he could see extended views of individual players. He watched a lot of Dennis Rodman and KG. They were great rebounders. Julian watched how they boxed out and exploded after rebounds. Dennis Rodman and KG both said it is a question of who wants the ball more. Julian stretched and did half his push up, crunch and sit-up quota and then showered and put on jeans and a hoodie to head to the welcome event. He ate and enjoyed the event. He noted that some of the top players in the state of Georgia and Florida were there. The coaches and organizers made sure that everyone mingled with everyone and there were no exceptions. Julian was an unknown and he kept it that way. During the individual conversations and introductions Julian simply said his name and what school he attended. He said that he wanted to get better as a player and that was why he was there.

Julian smiled a smile as if he had a "secret" like Kobe, MJ, Dr. J and others who were good and knew it smiled. They were like rattle snakes waiting to attack and devour you. Julian paid no attention to the guys bragging about their stats and stuff.

Julian took note of the silent ones who did not say or do much but just listened and nodded. Those were the ones he would have to look out for. It reminded Julian of the times he had watched the older guys playing in the park. There would be some guy in busted up clothes and sneakers looking "raggedy". One or two had even walked funny. They did not have the latest gear on or have the best clothes on. But once the game started you would then find out who they were. They would come out of nowhere and dunk on someone or out-shoot the entire team they were playing against. Julian figured he was going to introduce himself to the world by taking flight at this camp. That is what he intended to do. Julian completed the other half of his regimen; 50 each pushups, sit-ups and crunches. Julian caught a quick shower. Julian dressed for bed. He had a lot of "nervous energy".

He had brought an alarm clock from home to ensure that he was not late for events. He powered up his phone and told his Mom how his welcome to camp program had gone. He let her know that he was ok. She told him his Father said hi and to have a GREAT Time. Julian promised to learn all that he could and have a GREAT Time doing it. Julian felt in the end basketball was the same no matter where or at what level you played. He had heard the saying that no matter what **"Players Play"**. He had a "nervous anticipation" of the camp activities. He was not afraid to play against the other camp members. He just wanted to do well and let his game speak for itself. He was here to learn and learn some more.

He wanted to become better and had a feeling inside that he would. Julian knew at the end of the camp he could only get better for having come. When his alarm went off Julian rolled out of bed and said his prayers. Then he went to work on his sit-ups, pushups and crunches. Julian stretched for 15 to 20 minutes and then he packed his gear. Extra shorts, extra pair of sneakers, extra socks, Extra T-shirts, Lotion, sanitizer, cell phone, cell phone wall charger, Hoodie and sweatpants. He put on a plain black baseball cap. He had fallen in love with them and now had close to a dozen of the same cap. After a quick shower Julian dressed in his "outfit"; black tights for lower and upper body protection, black shorts, black sweat suit, black t-shirt, black sneakers, black socks and black wrist bands. Julian placed half a dozen extra sweat bands in his bag. He wanted to make sure that his hands were dry if he caught someone off-guard. He was going to make them victim number one on his **"revenge tour"**. After dressing and making sure that he had his room key, phone and gym bag he headed to the cafeteria to eat and then get ready for day one. He put his headphones on and powered up some old school R&B and took his time getting to the cafeteria.

Once Julian arrived at the cafeteria; he took a seat off to the side where he could watch most of the people as they came in. He went to the bathroom to clear his system. Then he got extra Gatorade and water and headed for the gym. Soon it was time for day one to begin. They started with warmups and then stretching.

After stretching the camp attendees were separated into clusters of 30 and then assigned to different courts. The groups ran layup lines and then free throw drills. Each person moved to the line for two shots. The other players were encouraged to make noise and stuff to distract the shooters. Julian did not participate in that part of the activity. When he got to the foul line; he hit all of his free throw shots.

Julian blocked out the noise, waving hands and did as Randall had told him. Focus on the rim, proper shooting mechanics, bend knees and follow through. Nothing but net on all of his free throws. While they were shooting free throws a voice came over the PA system. He said most basketball games are won or lost in two areas; the free throw line and rebounds. Think about how many, NBA, Semi pro, High School, College, NAIA, NCAA, pickup games and overseas games that are lost due to not getting that "big rebound" or missing those "free throws". The voice said the same thing that Randall had told Julian. Concentrate at the foul line. Take your time and use proper mechanics, bend your knees and come up through the shot and extend. Make sure that you follow through. The voice said a "major part" of Free Throw shooting is mental. You have to see yourself making the shot or shots. Don't panic. Take a deep breath and slowly let it out. You have to get in the habit of making your actions a ritual. One, two, three bounces, spin the ball, get the good grip, bend knees and come up through the shot, snap the wrist and extend after the shot. Practice, Practice, Practice and Practice some more.

The players on each court then began taking three free throws while at the line and then four and then five each. Afterwards it was break time. The PA announcer reminded everyone to remember which court they were on and to report to it after the 30-minute break.

The Camp organizers also had two medical stations set up in the male gym and the same in the female gym. They had oxygen, rolling stretchers, tent area and nurses on duty constantly. There were even ambulances outside the two gyms in case anyone was to get seriously hurt. After the break camp became fun. Each of the courts began to have the layup line contests. The two teams lined up; one on the right side and the other on the left side of the court. They would have to dribble to the other end of the court and make a layup and then get their ball and dribble back to the other end and make a layup and hand off to the next man in line and he would do the same. The first team to finish won. It was a fun contest because you quickly found out who could dribble and who could not. Some people dribbled with one hand all the time. The people who were strong dribblers dribbled down with one hand and made their layups easily and used the other hand to dribble the other way and make their layup then hand off to the next man. It was funny in some ways and brutal in others to watch people who could not dribble trying to quickly make it down the court and then make a layup. Julian's team lost but he did not care.

Well; he did kind of care; but he had found out that he could dribble the full length of the court and back with no problem using either hand.

Next the teams ran layup drills. Some guys took this opportunity to practice their dunks. The coaches did not discourage the players. However, players that missed one or two high risk dunks were told not to try it again during drills. Julian had to agree it got the energy up in the gym to see the high-flyers and their dunking. Julian did not dunk once. He laid the ball off the back board or directly into the rim. He wanted to break out his thunder dunk but he stifled the urge. He watched as one of the men on his court took Jordan's free throw line dunk and made it. Everyone was high fiving him; but Julian noticed that there were several guys who just nodded after he made it.

Julian felt that those were the guys that were waiting to sprout wings. Soon it was lunch time. People were talking about the guys that had made their dunks and the ones that had missed on their courts. Everyone was having fun with it. One of the guys at his table asked Julian why he had not dunked. He said other members of the teams on the same court had noticed how easily he had climbed high and just dropped the ball in the rim or high on the backboard.

Julian told them he did not dunk much only if he had to have a basket and someone was in the way. They all laughed and said they "pitied the fool" that would try to stop him on the run to the basket for a dunk. Julian just smiled as if to say he was going to see who was brave enough to try and stop his windmill, his side flight and his "Shawn Kemp power slam".

After lunch there was stretching on all courts. Afterwards there were dribbling drills. Then the teams competed in a cone dribbling race to half court and back to hand off to the next person. This time Julian's team finished first. The instructors held a coaching session on all courts on the necessity to "control the ball on the dribble". The Instructors demonstrated how the great ball handlers kept the ball on the dribble close to their bodies. They would use their bodies; not their hands for shields when making spin moves or bringing the ball behind their backs. The coaches demonstrated how they used their shoulders to get past people.

The coaches brought out extra basketballs and had each of the camp players dribble and they gave them pointers. They had the players dribble with their left hand continuously and then with their right hand continuously. The coaches walked by like the military drill instructors and showed those that were doing it wrong how to improve. The coaches did not try to embarrass the players. They did it in a playful way. They also took the time to dribble and show the players the difference. It was a great lesson and a fun time for all. After the dribbling drills it was break time again. After the 30-minute break the teams resumed shooting free throws again. One at a time until they had started shooting 5 times each. Then class was over for the day. Individual instructors would be available for two hours to help players with specific issues the PA announcer said. That was great news to Julian.

Julian grabbed his stuff and raced over to coach Ethan Greene who was coordinating the rebounding training. Once the interested players were assembled Coach Greene passed around a notepad for the players to put their names, phone numbers and email addresses on it. He would send the players tips from time to time as well as a copy of his blog. Coach Greene stressed to the players that there are only two keys to great rebounding. They are; "Will/Want and Position". He stated that these days players think because they are bigger or have a higher vertical jumping ability that they should get all the rebounds. He said it does not work that way.

Coach Greene said even smaller, skinny guards like Steff Curry, Klay Thompson and Chris Paul have outrebounded power forwards that are nearly twice their weight, taller, bigger and stronger than the three of them. He said the difference is that the taller players were counting on their size, length and verticals to get the ball. Chris Paul, Klay Thompson and Steff Curry wanted the balls more than the bigger guys. They would use positioning, desire and speed to win the rebounds. They had the will/want for the ball more so than the bigger guys. Coach Greene stressed to all the campers that first comes will/want and then positioning.

Coach Greene told all the campers that gathered around him to look up Dennis Rodman. He was probably the best rebounder in the history of the game. Forget his antics off the court. Forget his politics and just look at "his basketball game" alone.

Dennis Rodman would regularly outrebound centers and even whole teams when he played. He studied his team and he studied his opponents and their shooters. He noted how their shots would hit the rim or the backboard and their tendencies. He also was in tip top shape no matter how much he partied. He took passion in and really loved rebounding.

Coach Greene had the men pair up on each side of the court. His assistants would throw or shoot the ball and they would both attempt to get the rebound. Coach Greene stressed position and will/want. In his competition with Brian Williams who was the same height as him; Julian got some and Brian got some of the rebounds. Brian would also use a kind of football under and over move to get in position on Julian. The move by Brian surprised Julian. Brian did not do it all the time. He picked various spots to do it. Julian gave him credit for the move and asked him to show it to him after the practice was over.

Julian and Brian agreed to go eat dinner then come back to the gym and work on their rebounding before turning in. Coach Greene had the players go against him to get in position and he showed them how to counter other moves. He showed them how to "squat down" to maintain their position and be ready to explode upwards to get the rebound. He gave each camper that stayed a quick assessment. He told them of their good points and their bad points. He reminded Julian to stay balanced. He had lost out to Brian due to being off-balance or on his toes instead of dug in on his heels.

Coach Greene also commended Brian on using a football move to win positioning in basketball. Coach Greene bet Brian $10.00 that he had been a football player before or had a close relative that was one. Brian laughed and said you win. In Junior high and freshman year in High School I played both football and basketball. He gave Brian the $10.00 for being honest. Brian said, "Thank You" and stuffed it in his pocket. They all shook hands and headed to eat. Brian and Julian exchanged numbers. In the dining hall; while eating Brian said he planned to stay in the state of Florida and either go to the University of Miami or the University of Florida to play basketball. Brian said since he had dropped football his basketball stock was rising. He was now three-star rated. Brian said he had signed up for camp to improve his overall game. He had the grades. He was a B student with no major issues. Brian told Julian that he had come off the bench as first or second reserve for his ability to rebound and play defense. Brian said he wanted to become an all-around player and starter. Brian asked about Julian and his team. Julian told him the truth. He was the last man off the bench for his High School team.

Julian told Brian for some reason he would kill in practice but in the "games that count" he could not even catch the ball. He said he had been dating the leader of the cheerleading squad and had caught her cheating. He told Brian she did not know that he had seen her having sex with another guy. It had hurt for a while; but it was now the fuel that was driving him to be the best basketball player he could be.

Julian told Brian that he wanted to see if he could bring the practice Julian to the game floor. Julian said since "the incident" just over three weeks ago he had been practicing twice a day and watching DVD's of MJ, Magic, Larry, Steff, Klay, LeBron, Dr. J, Shawn Kemp, Bernard King, Dennis Rodman and others to get better.

Julian told Brian that his parents had bought him those strange shoes that are supposed to help you jump higher. Julian said, "they DO really work". He said before he got the vertical training shoes, he could not make a 360 dunk. He does so easily now. He said he also found a dunk that is his favorite and believes that he can do it from the foul line. Brian asked Julian what was this "favorite dunk"? It is called the "Shawn Kemp Power Slam". Shawn Kemp had this ridiculous vertical in his day. He would sometimes take off on people and put the ball behind his head with two hands and elbows extended out like wings. Shawn Kemp would power his dunk through the rim when he arrived there.

Then Brian said; "hide the women and children here comes THE HAMMER". They both laughed. After eating Brian and Julian headed back to the gym. They stretched for a while and then began working on their free throws 5 each at a time and then they began working on their jumpers and ball handling.

Since there were only a handful of people in the gym Julian decided to show Brian his Shawn Kemp power dunk. First Julian hit a 180 at full throttle. Next Julian showed his MJ Side dunk. He flew in from the side of the rim and reached over for the slam. He then hit the Dominique reverse slam with power and grace.

Then Julian unveiled his "Shawn Kemp Power Slam". Julian backed up past the half court line and took off running and jumped from the foul line. He put the ball behind his head with both elbows extended outward. He spread his legs like tail wings and threw the ball through the rim and to the floor "BLAM" was the sound the ball made as it hit the floor. The sound of the ball hitting the floor echoed in the gym. Julian gabbed the rim with both arms and did a pull up and then landed. The whole gym was quiet.

Unbeknownst to Julian someone had filmed the whole sequence of dunks on their camera phone from the nearby practice court. When Brian closed his mouth and regained his voice all he could say was he would hate to be the person trying to stop you on the run with that slam. They both started laughing and hi-fiving. Brian called it "THE HAMMER". They stretched a bit and then headed to their respective rooms.

"...Most Valuable Player..."

The footage of the "Mystery Dunker" was placed on YouTube and immediately went viral. Everyone wanted to know who the dunker was and where the footage was taken. No location was given. Twitter, Instagram and other social media picked up the footage and the numbers grew. The next day in North Carolina at the football camp everyone was talking about a dunker that almost tore the rim off with high flying dunk that was unusual. At first there were comments on the internet and social media that the person was MJ because the sideways dunk was just like Jordan did it in his DVD video Series.

MJ had to issue a press statement to say that it was not him as he could barely touch the rim now. He said whoever it was they had that side-ways dunk down perfect and he wished them all the success in the world and to call him. He wanted their autograph.

Now MJ wanted to talk with the "Mystery Dunker". The internet was ablaze with questions. The series of dunks in the video were studied and analyzed. The viewers said he had the power of LeBron, the flight time and glide of MJ and the agility of a young Vince Carter. Some thought it was the high schooler Zion Williamson that has made a name for himself as a dunker.

Everyone concluded this person was not stocky or thick built like Zion. The dunker was slimmer maybe a few inches taller than Zion Williamson. Randall Baxter got an email with the video of the "Mystery Dunker". Randall looked at the video a few times and then he rushed to his room to look at it on the bigger screen of his computer workstation. He had seen that power dunk before. He could not believe it. On video his baby brother looked like he could really fly. Well in reality he was. Wow was all Randall could say. Randall got chills as he watched the sequence of dunks over and over again. He saved it to his computer. Randall felt all jacked up for his camp and for when he returned home. Now he was glad that he had not beaten up Ron or had him beaten up. Now Ron Highland and Samantha White were going to eat lots of crow when the "Mystery Dunker" is found out. Randall did not trust his mother or father with this secret. He would keep this one all to himself.

Randall fed the flame. He sent the video to everyone on his contact list on all his social media except his parents. Randall watched the video of the dunks over and over again and he could see NBA written all over Julian with the way he attacked the rim for those dunks. Baby brother you are going to be a very rich man one day. Keep on working he said in a prayer to the heavens while in his room. Randall said a silent prayer that Julian would stay focused. He had seen the pain on his face the night that he had walked the 20-plus miles home. He had probably cried the whole way after watching the love of his life with another man. "God does not like ugly" was all Randall could say. He told his friends, teammates and other camp attendees about the video someone had sent him from the internet. He sent the video to everyone at the camp and asked them to send it to their friends.

Randall also knew he had better get to work on his football game or he was going to be working a 9 to 5 like everyone else. He had to develop the intense love and study of the game his brother had developed. Randall had a good shot of energy after seeing the video. His baby brother was now inspiring him to get better at his game. Randall began to study the great receivers in the NFL and find their strengths. Randall was not going to be showed up. He was going to "catch everything coming his way". He had to get better at running his routes. He was going to be the best receiver in the country or at least the best that he could be. Randall asked one of the camp quarterbacks to help him get better by practicing with him after each session.

"...Most Valuable Player..."

Now extra motivated Randall began to study film more, train more and analyze his game. He had to get better. He started a pushup, sit-up and hand strengthening program.

Brian and Julian met for breakfast the next day at basketball camp and each day after. They also ate lunch together and worked to help each other get better. They both gave critiques and suggestions to help each other improve their games. Or if one saw a move on video that they felt the other could use they would capture it on video and show it to the other one on their phones or lap tops. Each day after camp sessions they would go to the weight room and workout. Bench pressing and upper body one night. Lower body workout the next night. One day off to rest, use the whirlpool, tai chi, swimming pool and ice baths and then resume the training. The camp provided lots of GNC products to help the participants get stronger and lower their body fat levels. Working together Brian and Julian were becoming faster, stronger and better all-around basketball players. The coaches also reminded all players and participants that not only must they improve as players but as Men and Women.

"Respect is earned" was the mantra that the coaches and the camp coordinators kept repeating to the participants in both areas. Julian called his Mom and asked her to order a pair of the vertical shoes for Brian along with a couple of skipping ropes.

Julian gave his Mom Brian's full name, address and shoe size. The shoes and skipping ropes would be waiting for Brian when he returned home to Florida. Brian and Julian worked on their skipping rope technique at the camp. They took turns skipping in ten-minute intervals.

Julian and Brian were not checking social media. They had no clue or knowledge about the viral video of the "Mystery Dunker". Brian and Julian were busy trying to improve their games and hopefully their futures. They ran drills. They worked on their layup form. They worked on their free throws and mid-range jump shots. They would each have to shoot a minimum of 50 free throws and then 50 jump shots. They worked on boxing out for rebounds. They adopted Julian's program of 50 sit-ups, 50 crunches and 50 pushups. Each helped the other become a better dunker with tips and practice sessions. It was hard at first for both of them but gradually by the seventh and final week of camp they were hitting more of their free throws and jump shots. They were also excited because they were both named All Stars and selected for the All-star game. Brian was not taking part in the dunk contest competition, but he was rooting for Julian to place in the top three in it. The 24 members of the girls and men's All-star selections were all called up and given a gold medal and a plaque with their names on them. Brian and Julian could not believe their good fortune when their names were called.

After the All-Star announcement event the basketball floor was cleared for the dunk contest. Eleven men entered. It was two dunks apiece in each round. The top five scores would move to the next round and then the top three. In the first round Julian came out the gate with his reverse power dunk. He exploded to full extension on the dunk. It went straight to the floor. He made it to the second round and he uncorked his 180-dunk. Someone in the crowd thought the 180-dunk looked familiar and he looked up the "Mystery Dunker video" on twitter, Instagram and YouTube. It was the same motion and probably the same person. He told his friend that he believed Julian was the "Mystery Dunker" and showed the video of Julian's just completed dunk and the one on the internet. They began to pass the word to the other campers and coaches. People began to compare the two. Yes, Julian was the same length and build as the "Mystery Dunker person". They hoped that he would bring out the "strange power slam dunk" and then they would know for certain. Nobody was making that dunk. It was a sort of two or three old school dunks combined. It was the dunk made famous by Dr. J and

MJ where they would take off from the free throw line and glide to the basket for a one-handed dunk. Shawn Kemp had a two-handed dunk where he would explode for a two-handed behind the head power dunk. But no one had tried it from the free throw line. The "Power Slam Dunk" was different. People used the two-handed dunk one step off or three steps off from the basket. However, to take off from the foul line and instead of the one-handed dunk to "bring the thunder of a two-handed power dunk" that would combine power, flight time and grace.

For Julian ("the Hammer Dunk") was also a cathartic expression of his anger towards Samantha White and Ron Highland. Every time he went to the power dunk Julian recalled what he saw that night behind the gym. For Julian hammering that dunk home helped ease the pain.

It was Julian against Leroy Haynes in the finals of the dunk contest. Each man was given two dunks. Leroy won the coin flip and went first. His first dunk was a spinning reverse like Julian had done in the earlier round. He got mostly 8's and two 9 scores on it. He then went for a 360 dunk and missed. He settled for a 180-power dunk and got a few 8's and the rest 9's for difficulty and the power ending. Then it was Julian's turn. Brian ran over to him and told him to do the Air Jordan dunk from the left side and then down the middle with his power slam. They high fived. Brian reminded him now was the time to show them what he was about. Brian pushed Julian in the chest and told him show them; "drop THE HAMMER on them". They both started laughing. The encouragement and belief in Julian's abilities demonstrated by Brian made him stronger. That was the spark Julian needed. Someone really believed in him and his basketball game. He did as Brian suggested. Julian walked to the left side line of the court. He took a deep breath. He bounced the basketball twice. Then he started running he launched himself at the rim and turned sideways just like Jordan in his video and even gave the leg kick as he rammed the basketball home. "Blammmm" was the only sound heard in the gym as Julian landed on the ground. Then the crowd erupted. Straight 10's were the scores he received. He had nailed it.

Now for the monster thought Brian as he kept his fingers crossed that his new friend would blow up. Brian pointed to the half court line and then to the air above. "...Go Get...IT" he shouted to Julian. Julian nodded that he understood as the crowd was now realizing that Julian was the "Mystery Dunker". Julian took his time as he gathered himself. This one was to erase all the pain and hurt that Samantha White had caused him. He saw her and Ron in his mind as he stood past half court and stared at the rim that he was about to hammer. Julian took a deep breath and three bounces of the ball. He began running. At the foul line he launched himself toward the top of the square on the backboard.

Julian Jumped as hard and as high as he could from the free-throw line. Julian spread his legs wide and he put the basketball behind his head and spread his elbows like wings. Julian seemed to be moving in slow motion. He was flying. He flew from the free throw line with a scowl on his face. "He was going to tear this freaking rim off". Then he was there at the rim. Julian put all his rage and anger into this dunk. Julian let loose a primal scream of rage as he slammed the ball through the hoop and straight to the floor. The ball hit the floor like a bomb exploding "BLAMMMMMMMMM". The sound reverberated throughout the length and breadth of the gym. Julian hung on the rim with both hands and did a pull up before dropping to the floor.

Brian was yelling, screaming and dancing along with a host of other players and friends. People from all over the gym rushed to touch Julian. They shook his hand, patted him on the back and excitedly asked him if he was the "Mystery Dunker"? Julian did not answer.

"...Most Valuable Player..."

Julian just looked blankly at those asking if he was the "Mystery Dunker" with a question on his face. Finally, someone showed Julian the video and asked if it was him. Julian remembered the outfit he wore when he showed Brian the dunks. Yeah that was him. He pointed to court number 5 and said that was where he was. The crowd went nuts. They knew the "Mystery Dunker" that even the great Michael Jordan wanted to meet. The coordinators asked the crowd to move back so they could present Julian with the trophy. Brian came over to congratulate Julian and told him to enjoy the moment there were many more like it on the way for him. Brian and Julian high fived and then the presenter was there with the large trophy. They also gave Julian a check for $700.00 to go have a good time with his friends. Before Julian and Brian could get away it was game time. Brian and Julian had to play in the All-Star Game. Julian signed a few autographs and promised others that right after the All-Star game he would make sure that everyone got what they wanted signed.

The All-Star game began a short while later and news of the solving of the identity of the "Mystery Dunker" was all over social media, TMZ, ESPN, the sports networks, the news and the newspapers. Some of Julian's high school teammates could not believe that the person dunking like crazy with grace and power was the same guy on the end of their bench the year before. He was half-way decent in practice but in the game he just did not play well. The "New Julian" was on full display in the All-Star Game. Several times he took flight on other helpless players. Julian played with a reckless abandon. He had shed the shell of the guy who sat at the end of the bench.

Julian had the intensity of Michael Jordan, KG, Magic and Kobe when the game started. He was all over the place. Players thinking; that they were free for a layup or dunk soon found out how quickly their shots could be blocked or erased. Julian also showed that he could handle the ball in traffic. Brian rebounded the ball and fed Julian. Julian weaved through other players and elevated from the free throw line and power slammed the ball home. The crowd went wild.

Brian and Julian put all their rebounding lessons to good use as they secured rebound after rebound. They fed their teammates for fast break points. They took turns erasing shots with powerful blocks. Brian, Julian and his teammates over-powered the other team. To put an exclamation on his new game Julian even made his 360 on a breakaway. In the first hal of the fourth quarter Julian grabbed the rebound and took it over half court between two defenders and fed Brian for an alley-oop slam. Julian's team called timeout so that he could get a proper send off. The crowd all gave him a rousing and bleacher-stomping standing ovation.

The crowd whooped it up and yelled out "Mystery Dunker" as Julian walked off the court with a huge smile on his face. The scoreboard played the video from the internet and the crowd went wild as Julian was formerly announced as the "Mystery Dunker". As Julian came off the court his teammates high-fived and hugged him. Julian waved to the crowd and bowed in salute to the cheers like a conductor. Brian joined him on the bench. He and his other All-Star teammates celebrated and took lots of photos.

While waiting for the game to end Julian looked at social media for the first time and saw the responses to his video. He and Brian looked at each other in shock. To the surprise of no one; Julian was named Most Valuable Player of the Camp All Star Game. He was presented with a massive trophy and another check to take his friends out to eat. Randall sent Julian a note telling him to enjoy the moment as there were many more great moments coming his way. After the game a group of the basketball campers decided to head to a local Dave and Buster's restaurant to shoot pool and eat. They had a great time. Julian exchanged numbers with all of them. Many of them were surprised to learn that Julian had been sitting at the end of his High School basketball team's bench. They laughed and promised him that this year things would be very, very, very different. They all told him he would surely be on the starting five. Julian told them all thanks for the encouragement. He raised a toast to all the players there. Thanks for the encouragement from all of you and I send the same back to each of you. Wishing you all Lots of Success.

The teammates had a ton of fun and then it was one day of rest and back to their neighborhoods. The next day Julian and Brian worked out as usual then they went to the whirlpool area. There they talked about their plans. Julian said if things work out financially; he would be looking to join Brian in Florida at the University of Miami. He promised Brian that when he got home; he would look up info on the University of Miami Program and make contact with them. Brian and Julian shook hands and agreed to try to play together at the University of Miami the following year. The two ate, shook hands and hugged each other. They left for their respective rooms and travel home early the next morning.

Brian reminded Julian to unleash "THE HAMMER" on his opponents and told him that "the girlfriend thing" would take care of itself.

Brian told Julian that he would have offers from all types. Focus on your books, your game and your future. Remember those that cared about you from the start and your family. Brian also told Julian to never forget "US" poor people when he is in the NBA making tons of money. They laughed, shook hands, hugged and parted ways. They had to pack for the return trip home. After he had packed his main clothes and selected a pair of black jeans, black t-shirt, black cap, black hoodie, black sneakers and black socks to wear for the trip home Julian called his brother Randall. When he reached him; Randall was giddy with excitement for Julian. He told his baby brother that he was the "New Muhammad Ali". He had shocked the world and definitely rocked Marietta, Georgia. Randall told Julian how proud he was of him. He reminded him to stay grounded. He told him now that he was popular there would be a whole lot of people wanting to be his friend. Randall cautioned Julian to choose carefully and to take his time adjusting to his new-found fame. Randall reminded Julian to stay humble.

Randall said he was headed home early in the morning. He should be at the airport when Julian arrived. He would wait for him in the baggage section. Randall told Julian not to worry about calling Mom to get him. He would rent a car to take them both home from Hartsfield Jackson Airport. There was an Enterprise Car Rental place near their home. They could return the car there. Randall told Julian that the practicing and workouts at home were now paying off he guessed based on the video that he had seen.

Julian laughed and told his brother "so you saw it and never let me know about it"? Randall said; it's your time to shine but be careful, be vigilant and be smart about it. You have to keep doing what you are doing to get to the next level and then the NBA. Julian sat up straight in the stuffed chair in his room. NBA??? Randall told Julian point blank that he believed that he had the skills and potential to make the NBA. He told Julian; he needed to work even harder and play at least one year of College ball somewhere. Yeah it was a lot to think about thought Julian. After he had walked home 20-plus miles Randall knew his baby brother had determination and willpower in spades. Now he just had to keep harnessing his skills and talents. No, the NBA was not some "crazy pipe dream" for Julian. It was a future reality if he put in the work. Randall told his brother Julian that he loved him and would be waiting for him in the baggage claim area at the airport. See you there said Julian. He told Randall that he loved him and thanked him for the support.

Julian dressed and got ready to leave. He would get a large plastic bag to put his MVP trophy in. He would carry it on the plane with him. His gold medal, dunk contest trophy and All-Star plaque were in the travel bag along with the game ball. He had let the air out of it after having Brian, Coach Greene and a few others sign it. Then the realization hit Julian that the "practice player" he had always been had "come to the court with him" and now the two were one person. Julian would put air in the basketball when he got home and put it on his mantle place. He was a new player and a new man.

Julian headed to the Cafeteria and he was treated like a rock star. There was a huge round of applause when he walked in. People wanted to take selfies with him. People wanted his autograph and asked him questions about his game. Julian told them honestly that he had been the last guy off the bench at his High School. He laughed about it now and told the group that had gathered that he was so bad at basketball that his cheerleader girl friend had left him. Several members of the group said; "no way"! Julian said it served to be a "wake up call" for him. He needed to work on his game. He told them he practiced twice a day every day since. Julian told them between rest, eating properly and sleep he studied the best of the NBA and College and got better. He told the group that if he could improve all of them that wanted to be basketball, football or baseball players could improve their games too. Julian told the group that even if you did not want to play sports; say you wanted to be a computer programmer then you had to be "dedicated'. Study your craft. Put in the extra time. Arrive early and stay late. The whole group gave Julian a rousing round of applause. He took more photos and signed more autographs "Julian JB Baxter – the Mystery Dunker". Soon it was time to head for the bus to the airport. Julian grabbed a cup of coffee and orange juice. He would eat at the airport. He shook hands and signed more autographs and headed out. He kept the game MVP trophy with him. It was nearly 5 feet tall and heavy as heck. At the airport Julian checked in his suit bag and gym bag.

As Julian headed to his flight departure gate more people stopped him and asked if he was the "Mystery Dunker"? He said yes and took photos with some of them. Finally, Julian made it to his gate area.

Julian headed for the nearest restaurant. He asked them if he paid extra could he get some pancakes, eggs and sausages. One of the nearby restaurant servers recognized Julian from the internet photos and stories floating about him. He rushed to serve Julian. He told him that he had heard about his story. He promised that he would see that the chef made his order. Julian told him thanks and he was truly appreciative. The man who gave his name as "Kevin" rushed away to get Julian's order ready. He took over for the lady that had seemed hesitant to place the order. Kevin convinced the cook to get the pancakes ready. He came back and told Julian it would be just a few minutes. Julian ordered a large cup of coffee, creamers and sugar. Kevin asked Julian for his autograph and a photo. Julian signed and took the photos with Kevin. Kevin asked him the same questions the group at the camp Cafeteria did. Julian answered him truthfully also and said he was at the end of the bench on his high school team the year before. Julian told Kevin the same thing he said to the other group. He said he was such a bad basketball player and athlete that his cheerleader girlfriend had left him. Kevin could not believe it. Julian said it is true but look at me now. The whole country and the world now know my name and my story. Who is winning...now? Kevin told Julian that he was now winning. Kevin left Julian to get his order.

When Kevin returned with Julian's order and lots of syrup Julian told him that if you want to be good at something or improve your life you have to put in the time. He told Kevin that he now practices rain or shine six days a week. He told Kevin that whatever he wanted to achieve he could. He just needed to have a plan and put in the work. Be early and Stay late. Julian told Kevin the story that most coaches tell their players.

Julian said most coaches say that there is "A PLAYER" out there and you will meet him one day. He is working at his game when you are partying. He is working at his game when you are sleeping and also when you take a day off. He is working at his game when you are goofing off and when you meet him; he will "DESTROY YOU". Julian said for some of the players at the camp that did not practice as hard or as long as I do; they met a monster in me. Several of them I blocked their shots or dunked on them. Several of them I stole their ball and went the other way for a slam. When I was practicing; they were sleeping. When I was practicing hard; they were not practicing as hard. They paid the price. Julian showed Kevin the MVP trophy from the All-Star game. Julian told Kevin he could do or be whatever he wanted to be as long as he put in the work, time, planning, preparation, adjustments and continuous effort. Never, ever, ever give up on your dream Julian told him. Julian paid the bill and put an extra $50.00 on the bill for Kevin as a tip. Julian ate and then headed for his flight boarding gate. The attendant helped Julian get an aisle seat in the business class. That would give him room for his height.

Soon the Delta Airlines flight was in the air bound for Atlanta's Hartsfield Jackson Airport.

As the Delta Airlines flight moved through the skies Julian reflected on the way his life had changed almost overnight. Brian was right in that the work, studying and practicing had helped to change his life. Now his classmates, teammates and others knew who he really was. He promised to use his new-found popularity as a means to motivate, uplift and encourage others. He knew what it was like when he sat at the end of the bench as the games wound down and knew he would not play. Now, it was a new day. By now the coach had seen the video or heard about it. Julian was going to get his spot and his new number 13.

Julian made a note to go to the local sporting goods store and get some number 13 jerseys in black. The tears and pain were being turned to Joy in his life. Julian smiled ruefully and caught a quick nap before he got to Atlanta. Lord knows what awaits him there. He figured he would do just like he had at camp; walk straight through the challenges. He also knew that there were other players that would try to come at him and break him down. It was the same way in the All-Star game as guys talked a lot of trash; but Julian did as Brian told him to do. He let his game do the talking for him; 32 points, 14 rebounds, 8 blocked shots, 6 steals, 11 assists spoke volumes. The result = MVP of the All-Star basketball game. He was still growing physically. Julian knew that he still had to work on other parts of his basketball game, but he could now hold his own with anyone. Julian remembered what Mike Tyson would say "everybody talks tough until they get hit".

After his flight pulled into Hartsfield Jackson Airport Julian quickly grabbed his trophy and backpack. He rushed to meet his brother in the baggage area. Randall saw Julian first and began running towards him. Julian put down his trophy and backpack to give his big brother a "massive" hug. Randall commended Julian on his game and his look. Randall told Julian "now you have the confidence to raise up on any one and play your game". Randall told Julian that he had already secured an order for a Black Dodge Charger to get them home easy. Julian teased Randall that they would be looking like the police as they headed home. Randall told Julian that he had not thought of that but right now it might be the best thing for them. They both laughed and grabbed Julian's sports bag and his luggage bag and headed for the parking area shuttle.

As Julian and Randall headed out of the Hartsfield Jackson Airport parking area Julian began to come to grips with his new life. Randall told Julian that you are a "celebrity" now and can use that to get you a scholarship to the school of your choice. You can also use it to get you to the NBA. Julian told Randall that he was the third person to tell him that he could make it to the NBA. He said before he left for the camp Pablo up the street had said so. Then at camp his new friend Brian had said the same thing. Now he was hearing the same thing from his brother. All three of them could not be wrong. The NBA thought Julian. It would be a dream come true to make it to the NBA.

Right now, Julian was in the second part of Phase I of his plan. He had to make the team at his high school. Phase II of his plan was to get into the University of Miami and make their basketball team.

After he had completed getting into the University of Miami and cracking their starting lineup he would think of the possibility of the NBA. Julian believed in progressing one step at a time. It was how he had made it home from the school dance over the 20-plus mile walk. One step at a time he kept telling himself as he walked. Soon he was nearing his neighborhood and shortly after that he was home. Once he had conquered the High School scene; he would turn his attention to the College World and then the NBA World. Randall told Julian that he was proud of him for how he had conducted himself. He also reminded Julian to be humble and to act with grace when the confrontation between him and Samantha White comes. Randall said I know that a part of you wants to squash her and Ron like bugs. Focus on you and road ahead of you. Your future is bright with positive possibilities. You have your training regimen. Keep doing it.

Randall told Julian to remember to stretch constantly and take up Pilates and Tai Chi to keep limber. Keep studying the GREAT players of the NBA. Keep learning. Have the coaches look at your rebounding, your shooting your dribbling and give you pointers. Keep learning because you are sure growing. I feel like a midget next to you said Randall. They both laughed.

Randall and Julian stopped at a Chick-Fil-A on Cobb Parkway to eat and relax before heading home. Randall confessed he had not told his mother about the video. Julian said "Oh, Oh, Oh, Oh, Oh!!!!". If she finds that we have kept this info about the video from her; we are going to be in trouble with her and dad. Oh well said Randall it's already done.

They ate and then headed home. When they turned the corner into their subdivision there were a lot of cars parked on both sides of the road. It was Saturday afternoon and usually the traffic and cars are light and sporadic. There are not usually many cars around. A lot of people and their children are usually taking part in activities like track and field, softball, football, soccer and baseball. Julian and Randall both looked at each other and agreed "it was strange". Then they found out why as they turned onto their home street. There were banners, balloons, news trucks, kids, adults, reporters and neighbors out in the streets with signs. A huge banner read "Welcome to the neighborhood of the Mystery Dunker" and the image of a masked man with a cape like the superhero's Batman or Superman. Randall stopped the car and he just looked at Julian. They both started screaming with Joy.

Randall told Julian to get out of the car and to go and meet his fans. Leading the cheering were his Mom Angela Baxter, Rachel Sanchez and Pablo Jones from his high school. There were large banners all over the place. Julian got out of the car to rousing cheers. He pulled out the massive MVP Trophy and the crowd went nuts.

Julian bent at the waist and said "Thank You" to everyone for their support and the banners and stuff. He held up the MVP trophy from the All-Star game and told them all that this trophy is for each and every one of you. He signed T-shirts, banners, posters, photos and other materials. His Mom, Rachel and Pablo came up and shook his hand. They each gave him a "welcome home" hug. The news reporters and media captured it all. TMZ's reporter came up and asked him questions. He was asked if it was true; that he was not even a starter on his High School Basketball team last year. He told them yes it was true. He was the last person off the bench and seldom played. He said looking back it was because he was not taking the game as seriously and with the dedication that he gives it now. He also did not put in the work to get better before. Julian told the reporters that a "personal moment" had made him stop and take a hard look in the mirror. He had made the commitment to train twice a day since then. He said he studied the "Greats" of the NBA and with help from Pablo (his schoolmate), Randall (his brother in the car) and his Mom (who had been a basketball star in High School, College and the WNBA) he had improved his game. He said at the basketball Camp in Orlando he met Brian Williams and together they worked on improving their games. It was Brian that gave the power dunk that I do the name – "The Hammer". We are hoping to join together and play College ball for the University of Miami. The reporters and friends all laughed. One of the reporters asked him where did the dunk come from? Julian said the dunk is a kind of a hybrid based on Shawn Kemp and Dominique Wilkin's dunking styles.

The dunk combines the dunk from the free throw line that Dr. J and MJ made famous along with the power dunks of Shawn Kemp and Dominique Wilkins. One reporter asked what was the personal situation that spurred him to get better at basketball and where was his girlfriend Samantha White?

"Truthfully"; said Julian Samantha White left me for a football player. The whole crowd gasped; and they were all stunned. The reporter from TMZ asked what was the situation that made her leave you. To be honest said Julian "I don't know". I caught her with another guy, and I took that to mean she did not want to be with me. So, I changed my cell phone number, email addresses and took down her pictures and moved on. The reporter said she probably is sorry that she chose to leave you now.

Rachel and Pablo yelled "Payback, Payback...Lots of Payback...". They were jumping up and down. The cameras caught their act. Julian just laughed as did Mrs. Baxter and Randall. Julian said she wanted a star athlete and at the time I was not one. My dream now is to make it to the NBA and make my family, neighbors, schoolmates and true friends proud. Julian said honestly, I wish her well and I am moving forward and onward with my life. I want to spread the message that the disappointment of today could turn into a brighter future tomorrow said Julian. I want people to know that the kid at the end of the bench can change, can grow and can become better. My dream now is to make it to the NBA.

Julian told the reporters; "My dream now is to be the best basketball player, best human being, best man, best son, best brother, best friend, best neighbor, best schoolmate, best citizen, best teammate that I can be and leave this world with a message. He said I want all those that hear this story, read about it, be told about it to take away a few things. You never know what is inside of you until you try. Julian said his Mantra for life are three sentences. *"The best revenge in life is to live the good life. Make your haters your motivators and Never give in, never ever give up on your dreams".* One reporter asked what's next for Julian. First; say hi to my Mom, my neighbors, my supporters and then order a ton of pizza, chicken wings, sodas, water and stuff.

Julian told all those in attendance that he was truly, truly, truly touched and honored by the gathering. He said we are going to have a mini party right here. He called the nearby domino's pizza right then and there. Julian ordered 80 pizzas, 80 cases of soda, 80 orders of chicken wings, 80 orders of fries and 50 orders of sides. When the person taking the order asked for the name and location; Julian gave his name and street address. The guy on the phone said he was the Manager and had just seen his story on live TV. He said he was going to double the order free of charge and it was on the way ASAP. Julian paid his part of the check and then he turned to the crowd. He told them the good news about the food. Julian told the neighbors, fans and friends we need some music, some chairs and tables and we are going to have a good time. Julian told the friends, neighbors and fans that they were going to have a good old-fashioned block party. Someone find some music was the cry heard from the crowd.

Julian told them all that anything they wanted signed he would gladly oblige and if they wanted photos with him, of him or of the trophy – no problem. He was staying until the next afternoon if necessary. The crowd began to hoot, holler and yell.

Randall, his mother Angela, Rachel, Pablo and the neighbors all called for a group hug and they all hugged and high-fived Julian and each other. Neighbors blocked off the street with their vehicles. They left a lane for people who needed to leave to be able to leave. Soon various reporters were interviewing Julian, Randall, Rachel, Pablo, neighbors and school mates about Julian. They could not believe that the high flying and power slamming guy they saw on the video and in the video from the All-Star Camp game was on the end of the bench. Randall told all the media people (bloggers, newspapers, radio, tv, internet, podcasts) and others that "revenge is a heavy-duty motivator".

Randall told reporters and news people that Julian never once thought about or talked about beating up Ron or Samantha or getting revenge with violence. He took all his anger and energy and put it into basketball. He practiced day and night. In the midst of the celebrating Angela Baxter told Julian that he had a phone call. It was his father Andrew Baxter. He told Julian congrats on his success and he wished him much more success in life. Mr. Baxter stressed to Julian to let go of the past (Samantha White) and to focus on his future. Now that people know about you; they are going to be eager to try to make you look bad. He told Julian now you really have to work three times as hard at your game.

Mr. Baxter told his baby boy you also have to be careful what you do and who you associate with. Julian told his father he understood the responsibility and would not let him, the family or the neighborhood down. Andrew Baxter told his baby son that he was extremely proud of him and the man as well as the player that he had become. Mr. Baxter told Julian he had made him proud and that he loved him. He told Julian let me talk with your mother and you go enjoy your homecoming celebration. Have fun.

Andrew Baxter told his wife to call the Police and tell them what is going on and have them send some Officers over to make sure every-thing stays peaceful. Mr. Baxter told his wife to also have the Officers arrest Samantha White if she showed up also Ron Highland if he showed up. He wanted to have a peaceful time for his boy. Mr. Baxter told his wife to go spend an extra $300.00 on herself as she was spot on about Julian becoming a better basketball player. They both laughed. Mrs. Baxter said their baby boy Julian had already taken care of the extra expenses. He just spent $400.00 on a credit card that she gave him to order food for the neighbors and fans gathered here in the street. They both laughed.

Mrs. Baxter told her husband she was very happy for Julian. Yes, she would do as he instructed her and call the cops right after she hung up with him. Mr. and Mrs. Baxter exchanged "I Love You's" and hung up. True to her word Mrs. Baxter called the local Police station and told them what was going on with her son. They said that they had watched some of the broadcast on TV a short time ago. Mrs. Baxter told the Police Station Officer that she wanted to make sure that everything stayed peaceful.

She asked if the station could send some Officers to hang out with them. They agreed to send some Officers in exchange for a few autographs. Mrs. Baxter said that should not be a problem. The officer and Mrs. Baxter both laughed. The Officer said the men and women in blue would be there in a few minutes. He reassured Mrs. Baxter that there would not be any problems at the gathering.

Randall and Pablo both ran to their respective homes to get lots of sharpies and pens for Julian to sign stuff. Each man brought a bag filled with pens and sharpies back for Julian to use. They then went back to their homes for folding chairs, blankets, decks of cards, monopoly and other board games along with tables to eat, sit, play cards and have fun. One of the neighbors turned his stereo to a top 40 radio station and put his speakers on the porch. Then another neighbor added some more speakers to it and the party was on. Soon the food arrived. They all gathered at various tables to eat, play spades, poker, blackjack, board games and other card games. Julian sat at a separate table surrounded by Rachel, Pablo and Randall and signed everything that people wanted signed while answering various reporter questions. He received phone calls from TMZ, CBS, ABC, the Ellen Show, Tom Joyner Show, Steve Harvey Show,

Oprah Winfrey, The Wall Street Journal, Success Magazine, CNN, The Today Show, ESPN, MSNBC, The Atlanta Business Chronicle, The Miami Herald and The AJC Newspaper all wanted interviews.

Julian took his time and talked to everyone. The bloggers and other internet podcast operators were also given their time with Julian to record their stories. The Marietta Daily Journal Newspaper sent a team to the gathering. For Randall and Rachel the scene was especially gratifying as they had experienced Julian's "distress" the night that he caught Samantha White cheating.

Rachel recalled watching Julian go from table to table and group to group looking for Samantha White at the dance and she could not be found. Rachel felt and saw first-hand his pain and the extreme disappointment on Julian's face as he went from one end of the dance hall to the other looking for her. Julian did not care how he appeared to others he had loved Samantha White and she broke his heart. Now here he was receiving the attention and "star treatment" that he deserved. Rachel smiled as she watched the long line of fans, supporters, neighbors, classmates, teammates and strangers that were waiting for Julian's autograph. She echoed Randall's thoughts; "God does not like ugly". Julian had treated Samantha White like a queen; and she had repaid his love with betrayal. Randall felt great for his baby brother as he recalled the tear-stained and red-eyed brother telling him what he had seen at the dance that night. Randall knew in his heart he would not have had the courage to walk away. There would have been someone else also experiencing pain that night and every time that I saw him. Randall figured once this story got out Ron would probably be getting his "pay back" because a lot of people liked Julian.

On the other side of Metro Georgia Samantha White was being "introduced to that pain and payback". Samantha White walked into the local beauty salon and massage center to get her hair done.

"...Most Valuable Player..."

Every conversation stopped when she walked in. There was silence and many, many, many stares of pure hatred.

The minute Samantha White walked in all eyes turned to watch her. Samantha White was taken aback by the negative stares and negative attention that she was receiving. Normally she would walk in and wait to have a shampoo, treatment and styling by Miss Andrea. Miss Andrea was normally friendly, talkative and engaging when Samantha came in. Not Today!!! Today she had a look of pure hatred and hostility. Miss Andrea owned the large beauty salon and massage center. Samantha had been coming here since she became a teenager. Samantha White looked around saw the "up and down" looks and the other looks of disdain and hostility. She asked Miss Andrea what was going on? Why the spiteful and hateful looks? Miss Andrea said listen to this. She turned up the large 50-inch screens to high volume as the reporters talked about Julian and his "lost love". They talked about Julian turning into a monster player because he had caught his ex-girlfriend with a football player named Ron. Before Samantha could catch herself; she spoke. "So that was why he stopped speaking with me and avoided me. He saw Ron and I together"! I guess so; said Miss Andrea. My son and a bunch of their friends want to beat you and Ron up for hurting that boy. Julian was crazy about you Miss Andrea told Samantha. Even when he was here with my son tutoring him before he got together with you; he would bring you up all the time.

Julian's face would light up at just the mention of your name. At the very least you could have done was tell him it was over and not let him find out while you are with someone else. He saw you two!!! "It's females like you that give Black women a bad name. You cannot keep your legs closed. Females like you won't say no to other men and be faithful to one man". Miss Andrea told Samantha that she liked her before but now she needed to find someone else to do her hair. She was no longer welcome at her place of business.

The other staff members and customers began to let out a cheer and gave a rousing round of applause as Samantha White ran out of Miss Andrea's Beauty salon in tears. Every beauty salon in Metro Atlanta that Samantha White called or visited turned her down for service once she gave her name. Samantha White called her cousin Beverly at the West End Mall Beauty Exchange and explained her situation. Her cousin Beverly told her that she probably would not be able to get her hair done in any major salon in Metro Atlanta. The cousin told Samantha White they are all watching the stories about Julian and now your name is in the mix. You can come by my home at night and I will do your hair for you. That is the best that I can offer you. Other than that; you probably have to go out to Douglassville, Jonesboro or Lawrenceville to get your hair done Beverly told her. Pay with cash and do not use your real name if you want to try another beauty salon. Beverly told her the other problem that she faced is now that your name has come up in the "Julian Story".

The media probably have your picture in the stories and on Social Media. Beverly told Samantha that her best bet was to wait for her to do her hair at nights. Samantha White began to cry and full out bawl on the phone. Beverly finally told her very firmly to get a hold of herself and to stop crying. Her cousin Beverly told Samantha point blank you cheated on the guy. He saw you in the act and did not pull "a Rambo" on both of you. He waited and walked away. You were not crying when you were cheating on the guy Beverly told her. She said now the guy you cheated on becomes a star, successful and popular. Now your story comes out what did you expect?

It was at that time Samantha remembered Rachel telling her not to step out on Julian. Rachel had begged Samantha to tell Julian if she was going to see someone else. Foolishly she wanted a star athlete and left the superstar athlete behind. Samantha stopped crying and told Beverly that she would come by and get her hair done.

Julian called Brian to tell him what had happened on his arrival in the neighborhood as the pizza, chicken wings and other goodies arrived. Everyone there including the Police Officers began to line up and get food. The Manager of the Domino's Pizza had tripled the order as a tribute to Julian. People were taking pictures and others were also streaming the event live on social media. More people were showing up that had seen the event on social media or the news. It was a fun event for the entire community. It was all fun, games and good times to celebrate the success of a neighbor.

Randall, Rachel, Pablo and Mrs. Baxter all gathered around Julian for a series of group photos before he became overwhelmed by the neighbors. They all ate, danced, played cards and had fun. It was a grand time for one and all. Brian started laughing out loud when Julian told him what happened in his neighborhood. Brian told him what his brother Randall told him. Now you have to stand up and be counted. Carry yourself well on and off the court. Many, many people are now watching you. Brian said he was not worried about Julian being able to handle the pressure. Brian reminded Julian of his goal to get to the University of Miami and to leave the other schools alone. Brian told Julian that he knew that the University of Georgia, University of Florida, Kentucky and others would come calling. Julian told Brian thanks for the encouragement and support. He promised to keep in touch. Before he hung up Brian told Julian that he did not have to get him the presents; (the skipping ropes and jumping improvement shoes) that he found waiting for him at home. But thanks just the same. Julian told Brian no problem he was welcome.

Julian was so rushed by the neighbors and fans that he had forgotten to take time and personally thank Pablo and Rachel for their vocal support. He took a time out from signing to get a few wings, a couple of slices of pizza and a Coca-Cola. Julian sat down between Pablo and Rachel. He turned to Rachel and then to Pablo and told them each Thank you for their support, encouragement and assistance. He let them both know that he was very appreciative of everything. They all had a group hug and took lots of photos. The neighbors, fans and friends gave the entire group a rousing round of applause.

With the trophy on a bookcase behind him Julian, Mrs. Baxter (his Mom), Randall (his brother), Pablo (his best friend from High School), Rachel (a friend and supporter from High School), along with many others from the neighborhood, high school, junior high and elsewhere had a good time. They all ate, drank and celebrated Julian like he was a rock star. Julian received a phone call from Michael Jordan congratulating him. He also told him that if he keeps on working like he has done there would be room for him in the Air Jordan NIKE family. Julian's mouth dropped open and he began stammering. Then he regained his cool and he told MJ that he would "strive for GREATNESS" just as he had in his playing days. Julian was told by MJ that he was way ahead of the game because he had already weathered challenges and adversity. Jordan told Julian you had to know that deep inside you were a better player. You were killing them in practice but in the live game things were not clicking. Now add the work ethic and determination you have and here you are MVP. There is a lot more Success, Awards, Money and Good times ahead for you. Jordan told Julian it only happens "IF" you keep working, keep studying film of the NBA greats, keep an open mind and keep "dropping The Hammer on people".

Michael Jordan told Julian that he would be keeping an eye on him from now on. Julian told him "Thanks for the opening in the future. Thanks for the encouragement. Thanks for the phone call. I look forward to meeting you one day".

Michael Jordan told Julian it might be sooner than you think. Now the pressure is really on thought Julian. He said good night and hung up from MJ.

When Julian told Randall and the crowd who he had just received a call from the crowd went nuts. Now they were absolutely positive that Julian was destined for "greatness". The line for autographs and photos doubled after that announcement. Pablo, Mrs. Baxter, Rachel and Randall went in search of more markers and pens for Julian to autograph things with. Some neighbors also went home and got pens, paper and markers for Julian to sign with. Neighbors opened their homes so that other neighbors and fans could use their restrooms.

Another member of the neighborhood two-streets over from Julian heard about what was going on. He works for Waste Management Services Company. He called in and had his company deliver 12 Portable toilets. They put six at each end of the street. He also set it up for the Portable toilets to be picked up first thing in the morning. The Portable toilets had fluorescent markers on them; so that they were visible at night. They were all self-contained. Chemicals in the containers kept them from becoming stink after a lot of usage.

The nearby Publix Food store learned what was going on when one of their assistant managers saw it being streamed on the internet. They sent assorted chips, bottled water, sodas, ice, coolers, a variety of fruit and different flavor dips for the crowd to enjoy.

A local construction company brought several open top containers for people to toss their waste and debris into. People sat around. People played games. People danced to the music and other people ate to their heart's content. It was a "GRAND Homecoming" for Julian. As he told many people he would never forget this event. Mrs. Baxter told Julian that whenever he felt like slacking up or goofing-off she would crack the whip on him. She would remind him that he needed to keep making the family, friends and neighbors proud. Before the crowd dispersed signup sheets for names, phone numbers, email addresses and mailing address was sent around. They would be receiving thank you cards from Julian and his family.

Volunteers came forward and agreed to meet Sunday morning and clean up the area. There was a story of Julian's former High School team members talking about Julian and hoping that he would lead them to the state championship game. The former teammates said they were all working hard on their games to keep improving so that Julian would not embarrass them when tryouts came up next semester. The former team members were all starters last year. They admitted that if Julian played the way he played in the All-Star game at tryouts one of them was going to lose their spot. That person was going to have to come off the bench. However, if it got the team to the championship game; they had no problem with it. The team members said after seeing the tape and the tidal wave on social media they had decided to begin training right away. They had seen the video and had all gone to a local gym to practice.

One of the reporters asked the team members which one of them would try to stop Julian if he came at them with his "Hammer Dunk". They all said no to that one. Each one of them said if Julian took off on them for that dunk they were getting out of the way. They said you could see the rage and power being put into that dunk. One of the players said if it was him; he would grab Julian in a bear hug before he got off the ground and settle for the foul. That is better than getting jackhammered into the basketball floor. They all laughed. The reporters replayed the video of Julian dunking in the dunk contest. One of the Reporters on TV called Julian a "baby Darryl Dawkins, Dominique Wilkins, Kobe, LeBron James and Vince Carter" all rolled into one with a little MJ flight time spice on top. The crowd went to yelling and hollering again when they saw that report.

Julian spoke to the crowd. He told them that there was extra food, drink and stuff left and if anyone wanted to take some of the food, drinks and other stuff with them they had his blessing. He also invited those who wanted autographed photos of him, the trophy or both to email him. He gave them his new email address. Rachel and Pablo thought it would be a great idea to have a web site put together with training tips, interviews, updates and info on Julian. They would sell tapes, t-shirts and other stuff with the Mystery Dunker and donate all profits to the Boys & Girls club along with the Red Cross. They agreed to see about it. At 4am the Baxter's family (Julian, Randall and Mrs. Baxter) said goodnight. Pablo and Rachel left for their homes as well. They were all tired but happy. Julian hugged his MVP trophy even tighter as they made the short drive to their home.

Because of the crowd Julian and Randall had stopped right after turning onto their street. They went and retrieved the rental car. Mrs. Baxter called her husband right after getting them all into the house and letting him know what had happened.

They turned on the TV in the living room kicked off their shoes and relaxed a bit. On the news was a story of Samantha White running from hair dresser shop to hair dresser shop and not receiving service. Someone had video-taped her being turned down and sent it to TMZ and CNN. The other news outlets had picked up the story. Samantha White was now a pariah. Mrs. Baxter told Julian what other people had said when they learned of her story "Karma is a B_ _ _ _ word". They laughed as they watched Samantha White scurrying from store to store and mad women chasing her away and calling her names. There were all these "beeping sounds" as the language of the women was beeped out. Some women were seen throwing things after Samantha White as she ran out of the various beauty salons to her car and as she drove away.

There was a story of the University of Miami saying it would be in touch with Brian and Julian right away. They had already contacted the camp and received video of the two men playing games and working out. The University of Miami Coaches and Officials also said that they had received a copy of the tape from the All-Star Game at the camp. They were very eager to speak with both Julian and Brian about coming to the University of Miami.

The future home of the "Mystery Dunker" was put on social media and a web site by a University of Miami alumni.

The idea for the web site called "The Mystery Dunker – Official Site" appealed to Rachel, Pablo, Mrs. Baxter, Julian and Randall. The group wanted to encourage and uplift others and use the experiences of Julian. He had risen from the ashes of obscurity. He had dealt with challenges and worked harder to improve himself and his game. The idea really struck a chord with Julian as he recalled trying his hardest to get better as a player but going nowhere. Now, everything had come together for him. It could do the same for others if they keep focused, have a plan and they never give up. The entire package really appealed to Julian. Julian made sure to clear the matter with his High School Basketball Coach, Principal and the NCAA.

Julian and friends would retain none of the profits. They would donate everything away beyond expenses. The family attorney Mr. George Burrows wrote officially to the NCAA and the High School Association of Georgia to ensure that Julian would not be breaking any rules. The NCAA suggested that a Julian Baxter Non-Profit Foundation be created. In this way his intentions are clear "to help the community and youth" and not to enrich himself. Working with the family attorney the Foundation was formed and incorporated. In order to maintain his college eligibility Julian would have to be non-paid member of the Administration. His mother, his friends Pablo and Rachel along with a trio of Non-Profit professionals coordinated the venture.

The web site featured training tapes and feature DVD's on Julian. It also had a "life lessons" Program where other Professionals in sports, business and other areas would share their stories. Videos of the various dunks by Julian were being sold. T-shirts, caps, sweatshirts, hoodies along with stress balls were also being sold on the "shopping page" of the web site. There was also a "Request & Urgent needs page". People could request "Free of Charge speaking, meeting and appearances" by Julian. They would submit the time and location and the team would work to accommodate them based on Julian's schedule and the logistics involved.

Julian began to blossom and grow. His mother and father insisted that he complete an on-line Business Management course offered by Harvard Business School. To make sure that there were no excuses by Julian the parents pre-paid for the course. They insisted that Julian know he was now a "Brand and a Business Entity". He had to give as much as he had received. Julian's parents had a good heart to heart talk with him. He needed to understand that he was now living in a fishbowl. There are people that will pick at him and his game to try to make themselves look or seem better. Focus on you, your game, your future and remember how the neighbors, community and others are supportive of you and your success. "Go be GREAT"; his father Andrew told him. Follow the LeBron James model not the Michael Jordan model. They both are successful. Yes, Michael Jordan has more Championship rings; but Jordan never injected himself into community issues or took a side on anything.

LeBron and his Management team are very active and vested into the Black and Minority Communities. He is not afraid to take a position or speak out. That is something Jordan will never be known for. Jordan is known for his on-court skills and only caring about the Air Jordan Brand and the dollar signs. His parents urged Julian to remember first and foremost he is a human being. Second; "to whom much is given, much more is owed". His parents asked him to choose what his legacy would be in the community and the world after he has passed on in life. What did he want to be known and remembered for? Also, as a business-person he had to follow the Program of the best businesses in the world. He also needed to know that there were many people looking to see him fail. He needed to be mindful of that at all times. Julian was advised to pattern himself after the winners in the business world such as Warren Buffet, Amazon, Coca-Cola, NIKE, Delta, SunTrust bank, Chase bank, Kroger, Walmart, LA Fitness, Publix and others. Julian's father was still working with Lockheed Martin's "special projects program". He would go off for months at a time but remain in constant contact with his family to check on Julian.

To surprise Julian his father, Andrew Baxter took the red eye home for his son's first high school game since winning the MVP Award. His son was now being called "Julian The Mystery Dunker Baxter" by the PA announcer during pregame introductions. Mr. Baxter had heard and seen the interviews on the news, Radio Shows, Sport Shows, Oprah, Steve Harvey, Ellen and the Today show to name a few.

Mr. Baxter had been told by his wife that she believed the attention had not gotten to Julian's head. She said quite the opposite had happened. Mrs. Baxter told her husband that Julian went out of his way now to make sure that everyone received equal attention from him. He would sign autographs and speak with people until the last one had left. Mr. Baxter was surprised when he arrived at the gym. The Walker High school gym was packed and overflowing with people from the school alumni, the community, the media and those who had seen the video on the internet. Mr. Baxter could not help beaming with pride at the accomplishments of his "baby boy".

Mr. Baxter looked around and saw the banners from his neighbors, Julian's classmates, strangers and friends. It gave Andrew Baxter goosebumps. Mr. Baxter silently prayed that his son would live up to the hype and expectations. Mr. Baxter had also learned that the school (The Walker High School on South Cobb Parkway) had declined to allow Samantha White to be on the cheerleading squad for her safety, the safety of the other cheerleaders as well as to protect the school. There had been many death threats against her. The threats had come to the school in writing and on social media. There had also been threats on the life of Ron Highland and members of the football team that he was close to. A couple of them had ended up in the hospital for taking Ron's side in the Julian drama. There had been fights between them and people who believed Ron had done Julian wrong.

The Walker High School had a responsibility to take it all seriously. To be safe the school board and management had met and decided not to allow Samantha White to lead or become a member of the School cheerleading squad this year. Privately they hoped that she and Ron Highland would withdraw from the school and go become someone else's problem.

The radio and TV stations in Metro Georgia had also pleaded with the school to not to have Samantha White as a member of the cheerleading squad. They had received emails, letters and phone calls about the story. They felt it could or would incite violence from other people. The school board and the school management team agreed. The school had their attorney draw up a letter and sent it to her via certified mail. Everyone was relieved when it was learned that Samantha White had decided to leave Marietta, Georgia. She moved to New York where she had other family members. Many people in the school already knew that Julian was way ahead in his credits and could leave for College the next year. They wanted to see what he was made of. Many who had seen Julian sitting at the end of the bench the previous year wanted to see how much he and his game had changed. Boy were they in for a treat.

During the warmups the crowd let out a huge roar when Julian emerged. In both layup lines the players were showing off their dunks; not Julian. He soared to the rim and just dropped the ball through.

People in seats all around Mr. Baxter were talking about how high Julian was jumping to lay the ball off the backboard or directly into the basket. Finally, it was game time. The PA announcer left Julian for last and the crowd went nuts. People were stomping their feet, jumping up and down and making lots of noise. Julian was not on the bench for the start of the game. He was wearing the number 13 jersey and starting.

The other team, Wheeler High School had destroyed Walker High School by 40 points last season; not tonight. On the first play of the game; as the Wheeler player glided in for what he thought was an easy 2 points out of no-where came Julian to volley ball spike his layup shot into the bleachers. This was the "NEW Julian". Julian and his teammates became inspired to compete and then overwhelm Wheeler. When Julian took a rebound and raced the length of the court and raised up for his trademark "Hammer Throw down" dunk. The bleachers shook from all the people jumping up and down. You could feel the energy in the gym. Walker School began to press Wheeler full court. Assorted Walker players were given easy feeds by Julian and the other team members. They all played unselfish ball. At half time Walker School was up 18 points on Wheeler. After half time the rout was on. During a fast break one of Julian's teammates threw him a lob off the backboard. Julian caught it and cupped it in his left hand and windmill dunked it. Walker High School was leading Wheeler High School by 25 points. Some spectators even ran on the court with white handkerchiefs and towels saying; "the game was over". The PA announcer had to ask the crowd to stay in the bleachers.

When play resumed Walker continued to dominate Wheeler. Julian and his teammates had a great coming out party. Julian was on the run when the guard threw him a lob that they replayed over and over on the scoreboard. Julian caught the lob pass with two hands and turned 180 degrees and reverse dunked it. Once again, the crowd began jumping up and down shaking the bleachers whooping and hollering. Nearing the end of the game with the team leading by 30 points Julian was removed to more applause and jumping up and down. The team members were hugging and high fiving each other.

Mr. Baxter had tears in his eyes as he recalled the times in the past when he had come to the games to see Julian play. Most of those times Julian would only come off the bench in the closing minutes of a blow-out win or blow-out loss. He shed a tear of good fortune. His son had now become a star. He had a path laid out for him straight to the NBA if he wanted to. He had to finish this year in High school and then move on to college for at least one year and then the NBA.

Mr. Baxter knew that Julian now wanted to go to the University of Miami next year. The University of Miami had already sent information to Julian. Julian told them he planned to go to school for one year and then the Pros. They said they had no problem with it and had sent him the paperwork for a full scholarship next year. Brian had already received his package for a scholarship to the University of Miami. All their dreams were coming true. Mr. Baxter was thinking to himself as he watched the game end "God TRULY does not like ugly".

God was rewarding Julian with a taste of goodness for all the bad he had gone through with Samantha and Ron. Julian's father; Andrew Baxter applauded and yelled along with the other spectators when the buzzer sounded to end the game. Julian had demonstrated his skills in handling the ball, rebounding, blocking shots, passing and scoring.

Julian Baxter (aka the Mystery Dunker) had also soared above the "mere mortals" of Wheeler High School for 8 dunks. The guy at the end of the bench last year for Walker had transformed from Clark Kent into Superman. Now the whole world knew he was "for real". To escape the double and triple teaming the coach for Walker had had Julian bring the ball up as the lead guard. The Final totals for Julian was 29 points, 12 rebounds, 6 blocked shots and 11 assists.

Julian did not pay attention to the stats. He was only concerned that he and his teammates had won the game. The TV reporters, Newspaper reporters, TMZ, ESPN and others wanted to talk. Julian put on his warmups and grabbed a towel. He answered all their questions. Then he signed autographs and headed to the showers. When he emerged from the locker room there were still more people waiting for autographs. Julian grabbed a few pens and sharpies. He signed t-shirts, cards, photos, basketballs and people's hands "Julian Baxter – The Mystery Dunker".

When Julian turned to sign the back of a man's t-shirt the man turned around and it was his father; Andrew Baxter. His father gave him a big hug and pulled out his phone for a quick selfie. A nearby spectator took Mr. Baxter's phone and took a proper photo for the pair. The coach of Wheeler came over to congratulate Julian on a great game. He also shook Mr. Baxter's hand. The coach told Mr.

Baxter that if Julian continues to play that way now and in College he will become a very rich man soon. The group all laughed.

After leaving the gym with his Mother and Father Julian headed home to soak in the tub. When the family walked in there was a message from Rachel and Pablo on the family line voice mail. Shockingly there was a message from Samantha White telling Julian that she was so sorry for the hurt and pain that she had caused him. Julian quickly deleted Samantha's message. Time to move forward to the future and not the past. Julian called Rachel and Pablo back to say; "Thanks for being at the game and supporting him". He had seen them during the course of the game.

The school officials, school security, coaches from all sport teams, other players, classmates and the regular staff all worked hard together to ensure that Julian was protected at all times. Working as a team they kept an eye on Julian in class, between classes, at practice and during games. His classmates and teachers all helped him out where they could.

The season flew by. The team had only had two losses during the season. Julian did all that he could for the team. Sometimes he played the whole game as the season got closer and closer to the end. Julian and the team wanted to win their first state championship.

The Walker High School team won their division and moved into the playoffs. They crushed Marietta High School in the opening round. In the second round of the state championships they narrowly beat Alpharetta High school by 5 points. Next up in the semifinals they would have to play Altoona High School the defending champs in their division. This game was almost like a home game for Altoona High School as it was not too far from their school. All the Altoona High School students and their supporters showed up and showed out for the game. Altoona jumped out to a double-digit lead right away. Walker School fought back fiercely led by Julian and Adrian Townes a true senior. They combined for 29 points in the first half to keep Walker within range. Early in the second half of the game one of the Altoona players dunked on Julian and his team began cheering and applauding. The Altoona players began pointing and saying things to Julian on the court. The Altoona team was assessed a technical foul for taunting by the head referee after he had warned them to stop. A few minutes later he gave the team a second tech. Two shots. Altoona High was leading by 9 points. The Walker High coach called a time out. He told the team to play 1-4 wide. Meaning Julian would be the one to play the point. The other four team members were to play wide and the forwards and centers were to keep cutting to the basket. The forwards and centers were instructed to stay on the baseline and be looking for the ball at all times. The forwards were instructed to attack the rim. The Walker High School basketball team was instructed to feed Adrian and Julian as option one. The coach then pulled Julian and Adrian aside.

The coach told Julian and Adrian that if the team was going to the state finals now was the time for them to do their thing. The ball is going to be coming to you two; make things happen. The Walker team gave a quick cheer led by Julian "1, 2, 3 – WIN!!!". Julian went to the line and very calmly and coolly hit the two free throws. Now his team was down by seven. The Walker High School team decided to go to full court pressure. A steal and score by Adrian. Walker was down by five. There was an offensive foul charged to Altoona and Adrian fed Julian for a monster two hand throw down that silenced the crowd. The Altoona team was now up by only three points. The teams traded baskets and then another steal and 180 throw down by Julian and now it was a one-point game. The gym had gone deathly quiet as the teams traded baskets. Then with three minutes left the Altoona team fell apart.

After a rebound and pass by Julian to Adrian on the run up the floor one of the Altoona players tripped Adrian and then tried to grab the ball. He was given a foul for the tripping and a technical for arguing the call. The replay on the big screen clearly showed that the tripping was intentional. There was an official's time out. The Altoona team was over the limit for fouls. Adrian had to take his two shots and then the one shot for the technical was to be taken. Adrian missed the first of his two shots. The second shot by Adrian spun out. The Walker team was still down one point. Next, Julian stepped to the line for the technical shot; nothing but net on the shot. Walker was now tied with Altoona as the clock was winding down in regulation time.

It was just under one-minute left in the game. The Altoona team came down and spread the floor. They wanted to score and leave as little time on the clock as possible. Their best player took control of the ball and tried to go one on one with Adrian. As he launched towards the rim for an uncontested layup Julian left his man and jumped up to meet him. He blocked the shot and Adrian quickly grabbed the rebound. It was now under 20 seconds left in the game. This was no time for a time out. Julian sprinted into the front court. Julian pointed to the top of the square and called for the ball to be thrown high above the rim. With Julian ahead of him Adrian brought the ball up-court as fast as he could. They both raced to the other end of the basketball court at top speed. Adrian crossed over one defender and outraced the rest. Adrian had seen Julian go to the top of the square before on one of his dunks. As soon as Adrian got over the half court line a few steps he lobbed the ball towards the top of the square above the rim. There was a hush over the gym as Julian raced to catch up with the pass. He extended his right hand back as far as he could and caught the ball. In one motion Julian threw the basketball straight through the rim and to the floor "BLAMMMM". Seconds later the buzzer went off. Walker High School had escaped with the win. You could hear a pin drop in the gym for a minute as the replay showed on the scoreboard. Then all hell broke loose. Julian had scored in time. There would be no overtime. The small group that had made the trip from Walker High School began cheering and running onto the court. Even some of the Altoona fans cheered and clapped because they had witnessed a player not wanting to lose and giving an all-out effort. The crowd chanted Julian's name. The Walker High School team rushed to their locker room and quickly dressed. They were tired and wanted to be headed back to town. The last shot by Julian was shown over and over on the scoreboard.

The game was played near Northern Alpharetta so it was going to be a long trip back to Marietta. Once they got on the bus most of the Walker High School team members including Julian put blankets all over and around themselves. Each of them grabbed the pillows and went to sleep. They had been in a brutal and physical war. Although tired; the team was all smiles because they had won. They were going to the state finals at Georgia Tech gym in two weeks. Right now, the starters and main substitution players were battered, bruised and tired.

The coaches let them rest and sleep. They made sure that all of the players were comfortable. Coaches ensured that each player put some Gatorade and water in their systems. They did not want any players to cramp up. The coach himself made sure that Julian and Adrian were all snug with blankets around their entire bodies and lots of Gatorade and water nearby. Right after the game the team coaches began forcing Julian, Adrian and the players to drink large quantities of Gatorade and water. The coaches could all be heard going through the Walker team players locker room yelling "Hydrate and Gatorade". At first the players laughed and then they understood the seriousness of his message. When the adrenaline of the game died out and fatigue set in the cramps would come to the legs, arms, and lower back areas of athletes. Some players did not even shower. They put on dry shorts, dry underwear, dry t-shirts, dry socks and a sweat suit. They became "dog tired". The Gatorade helped with the recovery process after lots of exertion.

As the team rode back to Metro Atlanta Mr. Baxter was doing a "jig" to the tunes on the radio at his job.

Mr. Baxter was excited as he read the email about his son's performance from the coach. He had to be careful and not make too much noise as he was in a top-secret Lockheed facility called "Skunkworks". Mr. Baxter sent an email to his wife about Julian and again thanked her for the job she was doing in safeguarding Julian. He ended his email by stating that he loved her. Julian went straight to sleep as soon as his head hit the pillow. He was gone. He had spent all his energy on the game. If the team did not make the finals it was not because Julian Baxter had not given his all trying to win.

Julian had all season long led by example. He was never the "Rah, Rah type". Julian simply gave an all-out effort every game. When he played; he really played. He leaped into the bleachers, jumped over tables and dived on the floor at times to secure a win for his school. He had gone to great lengths to erase his team member mistakes in letting someone free. In the same way he had stretched to make hard layups and dunks he had done the same to block or alter shots by opponents. Julian had learned the art of the chase down block from Kobe, MJ, Shawn Kemp and LeBron James. Now it had all paid off as the Walker High School team was going to be playing in the state championship game. Julian fell asleep with a smile confident that he had given his all. He had not had time to speak to fans. He was totally exhausted. He drank Gatorade and Water as instructed by the coaches. He slept with a smile on his face.

The team rode home in silence as the lead players, coaches and others tried to get some rest. It would be rest time until Wednesday when practice and preparation would begin for their next opponent. The team would be playing Johnson High School out of Savannah.

The Johnson High School team had won their game earlier in the evening. Monday the coaches would begin working on scouting the Savannah team and looking at their top players and others. The coaches would look at film and player stats. The Walker High School team players would have Monday and Tuesday to rest and recuperate. Then Wednesday the team would begin looking at film and reading scouting reports. By the end of the week the team would be implementing plays to offset the strengths of Johnson High School. Any adjustments in the planning and plays to be used against Johnson High school would take place the week of the big game.

The coaches at Julian's High school would have to revise their plays for the next game. Their opponents were a solid defensive team and to take Julian out of the game may go to double teaming him. Where would the Walker High School team go for their other points? The Walker High School coaches had never implemented the 1-4 spread offense before with Adrian roaming the baseline and Julian handling point or vice versa. Everyone else had gone wide. The other team would know about that play. They would have to come up with something different. Everyone else will have to be either good shooters or people that attacked the rim if the other team double teamed Julian. Midrange and layups would be available to them if the team sent two people towards Julian. Adrian was going to be one of the primary other weapons. Mark Williams was a streaky shooter but could hit from three-point range and was very deadly from the midrange area. The coaches figured they would need to focus their practice on the mid-range shots. They would have to remind the whole team to step in when the double teams start. If your man left to double team someone; move in closer for a shot.

Mark Williams could find the space the other team would leave to double team Julian. They could still run the 1-4 spread with Julian running the point. When the double team came Adrian would cut to the center lane or get the lob and Mark Williams would cut to the free throw line area. That could work said the coaches. The other adjustment would be to play a 3-2 with Julian on the baseline with Adrian. Get the ball to Julian before the double team gets there. It is harder to double team on the baseline area.

The coaches also figured that they needed to take the fight to the other team. They had thrown Wheeler High off by pressing continually in the first half. They would do the same to Johnson High.

The team would full court press from the start of the game to the end. Just like they did with Wheeler High School. Besides this was the last game of the year and for all the marbles. They would have the whole summer time to recover. The coaches would need to review the film they received on their next opponent.

Julian was still asleep when the busses rolled into the school parking lot. The players awoke to the band playing and large crowds with banners welcoming them back. The crowd roared and cheered as the team came off the busses. The team was recharged by the fact that the fans had come out in full force to welcome them back. Adrian spoke for the team Thanking all those that came and those who; "were physically absent but present in the spirit" because it was past their bed time. The crowd roared with laughter.

Adrian told the crowd it was a tough battle but we are on to the Championship game in two weeks. Do you believe that we deserve to win the championship Adrian asked the crowd? They started yelling back Yes, we do and hell yeah we do! The coach came to the mike and thanked everyone for coming out and supporting the team. He said that he and the team were going to need all the support that they could get for the championship game. Coach teased everyone by saying he was looking at the faces around and he had a photographic memory. If he did not see those same faces at the championship game; he was coming to your home to get you. He replied just kidding. I have a hard time remembering the faces of my players and their names. Everyone started laughing.

Coach said "seriously folks" we are going to need all the support that we can get at the championship game. They all yelled they would be there for the game. The championship game will be held at the Hank McCamish Pavilion on the Georgia Tech Campus. The crowd gave the team a loud round of applause. Family members gathered their players and they all departed for home to rest and get ready for the next week of classes and practices.

Meantime in Florida Brian sent a text and email when he learned that Julian would be in his championship game. He congratulated him on his team winning. Brian told Julian now you have to be really ready for war. The next team is going to try to keep you and Adrian your teammate out of the score book.

Brian said you are going to have to serve as a main decoy for the other team members to score and get the points. Your team has to be ready to fight to the finish just like the last game. Its "HAMMER TIME" Brian told Julian. You have to find a way to get a massive throw down to kill the spirit of the other team. Julian emailed back thanks for the info to Brian and he told him he was always ready to bring "THE HAMMER". Brian wished Julian good luck and said he would be praying that things go well for him.

Julian rested as much as he could. He just stretched and rested between and after classes. He went to the whirlpool, sauna and had several massages at the Massage Envy Spa near his home. He drank a lot of GNC energy drinks, lots of water, ate fruit, salmon, seafood, baked and grilled chicken. Finally, Wednesday arrived; Julian put on sneakers and equipment to practice for the first time since the game with Altoona.

The coach made sure that all the players warmed up and then stretched. Then they ran layup lines and shot free throws for the first hour of practice. Then a tape of a couple of plays were shown from the last game. The coach wanted to show the players where they expect the gaps to be. Julian was at point and Adrian had run through the lane near the foul line. The coach showed the change he expected the team to make for the coming game. Julian would run the point. Shooters to either side of him have to be ready to step into the gap when they double team Julian. The double team will come mostly from one of their other guards. From time to time the other small forward or the center would try to double-team Julian.

The coach also pointed out that Adrian and the other forward would now have to run the baseline instead of near the free throw line.

The coach said this team will be hitting all of you all the time. It will gain you nothing by whining. Let me say this again "Whining about the other team hitting and grabbing you will get you nothing". Getting upset and retaliating will cost you game time and the team could lose because of it. You must take the ball hard to the rim. This team reaches a lot. You will be fouled all game long. The coach told Julian if he was feeling his shot or if he could attack before the double teamer reaches him he had the green light. The coach also said to Adrian, Julian and the other forwards be ready for them to step in to try and get the charge call. The team then began to run the 1 – 4 wide play but instead of settling for long shots the shooters cut to the foul line areas and got the 13 to 15-foot shots. The coaches were all pointing out proper spacing. The team took a break to hydrate and stretch some more.

The coaches then had the players work on their full court pressure with reserve players and coaches trying to break the pressure. After 45 minutes of that the team took a break to look at the film. They were getting beat with the long passes and no one was quick enough to intercept or jump them. It would have fouled out several of the team players if it was the game. The coaches figured it was front pressure that was lacking. The front three had to be aggressive so that the other team will make mistakes. The coaches showed the film of the Wheeler game win.

The coaches pointed out how aggressive the front three had been in demolishing Wheeler. The coaches said if they could free up Julian or Adrian to throw down a rim rattler on this team it would shake them up. For the rest of the time until the championship game the team worked on their full court press and free throw shots.

Halfway through the last day of practice the coach blew the whistle to stop practice and inform the team that they had two special guests. It was Dwayne Wade and Ludacris the rapper. Ludacris told the team that the future was in their hands. He said he was just a store clerk with a dream. Now he is living that dream. He told the team they have to believe when they take the court that they are there to take home the trophy. He said when I take to the microphone I know that I am able to handle my business. When you take to the court you have to be ready to send a message. Then Dwayne Wade stepped up. He said to win in a championship it is the one with the "heart" that is prepared to impose their will that will win. Dwayne Wade told the team like Ludacris just told you; you have to be ready to handle your business. Hit your shots. Hit your free throws and go to the rim hard. Give everything you have and you win. Save some for later and you will be sitting on the sidelines while the other team takes home the Championship game trophy. Dwayne Wade and Ludacris both echoed what the coach had been telling the team. The team gave them both a loud round of applause.

"...Most Valuable Player..."

The coach told them to get their rest and the busses head out to Georgia Tech and the Hank McCamish Pavillion at 10am the next day.

The Coach told all the team members to "Be ready". Julian pulled Adrian aside and Mark Williams their best shooter from outside. Julian told both men that they were going to have to carry most of the scoring load. Get ready for a war that we will win. Believe that; he told Mark and Adrian. We are going to win because I am dropping "the HAMMER" on them. I need the chance to hit them with one shot early and then another to break their will. They shook hands and headed home. Julian raced home to look at tape of the Wheeler game. They had been calling out signals to each other and making sure that the double-team traps worked.

In the two losses they had not called out the movement and lockdown traps to each other. Julian said to himself they damn sure would be calling the lockdown traps out in this game. They would bring the pressure like one former coach in college said; "it is going to be 40 minutes of hell". Julian went to sleep right after he hit the bed. His father had already called and wished him good luck. His mom was nervous. Julian knew his family wanted him to win this game more than any game in his young life. He would do as he usually did; give it his all. Julian always played to win.

Early the next morning Rachel, Pablo and a lot of students pulled up to Julian's home to give him and his Mom an escort to the school. Mrs. Baxter would be driving to the game behind the three team busses. Julian always travelled with the team. He was no prima donna.

The Walker High School team gathered and had a quick pep rally and then headed towards downtown and the Georgia Tech Hank

McCamish Pavilion on the campus. They had a team of Marietta Police escorting them on motorcycles and in cars.

At the Georgia Tech basketball gym the team had a quick prayer and meeting. The other team has "the experience" but they have never experienced "THE HAMMER" or our full court press experience. Get loose, Get taped up and let's take this trophy back to Marietta. The national Anthem was sung and then the players were introduced. Then the game began. The Johnson High School team was long (their shortest player was 6' 6") and could shoot. They took advantage early and were up 8 points in no time. Mark was the player on fire for Walker High school as Julian got him three easy shots in a row.

Mark kept them close until half-way through the first half. Adrian got an alley-oop from Julian and then the flood gates opened. The full court pressure by Walker High began to work. Mark found Julian on the run and he rose high and hit Johnson High School with a "THUNDEROUS SLAM". The crowd rose to their feet as they felt something had changed. There were three more quick turnovers and three quick buckets with Julian flipping in a blind reverse shot after being fouled on the way to the basket. Julian stepped to the line for the free throw to give his team a seven-point lead. Nothing but net. The other team called a timeout.

Julian's coach said if we can get another run like that one; we will win. They will go into the locker room upset and with no answers. They had played very well and now are trailing. They will be confused.

Gregg Randle, the coach said to Mark and Julian. They are double teaming Julian. When Julian passes to you they back off of Julian. When Julian passes to you for the shot hold the ball. When Julian's man backs off throw it towards the top of the square. That is Julian's territory. He'll go get it. Julian and Adrian started laughing and shaking their heads. Adrian told the team get ready for "the Hammer to drop". After the time out Adrian grabbed the missed shot by Johnson High and raced up the court. He found Mark and just as coach had said once Mark got it the extra man guarding Julian backed off to go double team Mark. Mark took one dribble and let loose a long lob to Julian. Julian raced to catch up with the lob. He put the ball behind his head and spread his legs as he flew towards the rim. This one was for Ron Highland and Samantha White thought Julian as he powered the ball through the rim straight to the floor. BLAMMMMM was the sound the ball made as it crashed to the floor. Julian spun away from the rim and raced back to his position to apply full pressure to Johnson High. The lead swelled to 22 and mercifully the half time buzzer sounded. At half time coach Gregg Randle told his team to make sure and get your ankles taped again and fresh socks. Get some rest.

The coach told the players in the second half "The starters will stay in". He reminded the team that when you get someone down you keep them down. Coach Randle told the players like John Thompson, the famous coach at Georgetown would say; "Never let up on someone. You never know what could happen".

Coach Randle told his team that the Johnson High School team was going to come out angry and ready to fight. Let your play do the talking. Mark was told by the coach to shoot like his life depended on it. The coach huddled with Adrian and Julian. He told them to be careful as the players may try to undercut one or both of you if they see you going to dunk on them. Be ready to change plans or stop and pull up for a shot. Sure enough; right after the second half started on the break Julian got the ball and a player from Johnson High went to undercut Julian. He took off anyway. Instead of going straight at the rim he cupped the ball and spun away from the player and reached over him to dunk the ball. The crowd went crazy. Adrian high-fived Julian as he ran up court to get back on defense.

The two teams traded buckets for the better part of the second half. Then once again the full court pressure got to Johnson High School. One quick pass to Adrian for a dunk. One quick turn over and a long three pointer by Mark. Another three-pointer by Paul Treco on the other wing and a windmill dunk by Julian over two players killed it for Johnson High School. The three men jumped. The two Johnson players seemed to stop climbing as Julian went a floor higher and windmill slammed the ball through the hoop over them. Just like his favorite player "Shawn Kemp" used to do in the NBA. Some spectators ran onto the court waving white towels screaming; "Johnson High School gives up". "They can't take any more beating". Security had to remove a group of the spectators. The lead was now 32 points for Walker High School.

For the Walker High School basketball team there was no celebrating. They were still intense and totally focused as the coaches continued to give instructions. Exactly three and a half minutes later the game was really over as Julian beat his man and took off from the foul line for his "THE HAMMER DUNK". He watched as a man started to come to take a charge and then changed his mind and bailed out. Julian dropped the hammer on the Johnson team and the bleachers exploded as the crowd started jumping up and down screaming the "Mystery Dunker strikes". With 4 minutes left in the game Coach Gregg Randle pulled his starters and put in substitutes.

The five starters came off the court to thunderous applause. The bleachers were shaking as Walker High School fans jumped up and down in celebration. The handcuffs were off the Walker High School team players now. They began to hug each other, smile, high-five and cheer on their other teammates. Soon the game was over. Julian and the Walker High school team had become the State of Georgia Champions. There was hollering, shouting and hugging all over the Georgia Tech arena.

"...Most Valuable Player..."

Julian was named MVP of the game. He was given a huge trophy and a medal. Julian was also told he would be receiving a ring for being named MVP. The whole crowd started chanting "Mystery Dunker" when Julian received his trophy. The team members were each given gold medals for winning. Every member of the team and the coaching staff would all receive their own individual championship rings.

The team members and their coaches would also all receive smaller versions of the Championship trophy. The team and fans jumped in their cars and headed to Walker High School's gym. There was going to be a party in the gym. The PA announcer made an announcement of an all-night party at the Walker High School gym for the new State Champions.

Although it was a tiring game because of the full court pressing the team was energized by the fact that they were now State Champions. Julian had just received his second MVP trophy. Randall and Brian were right. There were more great moments coming his way. In a convoy the team and their fans escorted by the Marietta Police raced back to the Walker High School gym. When the team and their fans arrived at the gym it had been decorated with banners and signs proclaiming the school "State Champions". A DJ was cranking up the music. There was lots of food, snacks and drinks. The coach; Gregg Randle was running around high-fiving everyone. He had shed his jacket and tie. He had rolled up his long-sleeved shirt. Once the party started the coach went to find Julian. He told him in front his family and friends that he is proud of the man and player that he has become. He said it may have been a tough situation with Samantha White and what you experienced. However, you need to know that no matter what; the talent, drive and skills were always inside you. At some point the practice player and the game player were going to become "the whole man". Coach Randle said he saw Shawn Kemp and MJ play live and you are making both men proud with your "HAMMER TIME" dunk. He thanked Julian for his efforts this past season. He said no Julian and no State Championship.

Coach Randle wished Julian well in all his future endeavors. He said Julian could call him anytime. They hugged and shook hands. Coach Randle told Julian to "Go Be GREAT". He left Julian to visit with the other players. Coach Randle already knew that Julian was going to leave school early and head for College.

After the coach left him Julian and his teammates said tomorrow would take care of itself. Right now, they were going to enjoy the moment. They were the State Champions in their division. Randall called Julian and told him Congrats as did Brian. Rachel and Pablo were right there at the game cheering Julian on. Terry Hall, Coach of the University of Miami Hurricanes basketball team called Julian to congratulate him. He said he hoped and prayed that Julian would accept their full scholarship offer and help them put the Hurricane basketball program on the map. Julian told him he was looking forward to it along with his pal Brian. Michael Jordan called to congratulate Julian and told him that he was still keeping a close eye on him. Rachel, Pablo and classmates all came by to give Julian a hug and shake Julian's hand. They all congratulated him on being named MVP again.

Most of them knew that Julian now wanted to be in the NBA. The next stop for him would be the University of Miami Hurricanes Basketball team. Mrs. Baxter came over and gave Julian a big hug and whispered to him to enjoy the moment and savor the victory. She told Julian to analyze the game afterward just like you would a loss. She urged Julian to get in the habit of analyzing both his wins and losses in life equally.

Mrs. Baxter reminded Julian that as many of the top leaders, top warriors, top sports stars said you have to learn from everything.

You learn more from the defeats but there are lessons to be learned every day. Mrs. Baxter said she was very proud of the man that Julian was and the steps that he was taking. She told him to have fun and enjoy the moment. Julian and friends danced, partied and ate until the wee hours of the morning. There were volunteer drivers to take players and family members home. Rachel and Pablo took Julian home and reminded him that he needed to record an interview with them for the web site. They set the time for later in the evening the next day after Julian had recovered.

Pablo and friends had recorded video of the game, the trophy presentation and the celebrations. It would all go up on the web site in the morning. They all said good morning as they dropped Julian off at his front door. Julian dropped his backpack and gym bag in the living room and climbed into bed. He took off his hoodie and sneakers. He was out like a light. He had faded to black in no time at all. His mother came into his room to check on him. He was face first stretched out across the bed. She got a large sheet from the closet and covered him up. She stared at him and smiled. He had come a long way in such a short space of time. Mrs. Baxter closed the door to Julian's room quietly and headed back to bed. She had always thought that Julian would become better at basketball but "this good" to become state champion no way did she see this coming.

Now Julian had aspirations of being in the NBA. Oh well, time will tell she said as she took off her robe and climbed back into bed. If he had the determination to walk 20-plus miles home to avoid someone after a traumatic situation then; anything was possible for him. Mrs. Baxter smiled as she thought of her husband's reaction when she had first told him that Julian might have a future in basketball. He had asked her if she was "confused" and talking about Randall. Now that Julian had been named MVP twice and has a full basketball scholarship to the University of Miami; he was going to have to eat crow. He was in the same boat as Samantha White. They were both guilty of not having faith in Julian. Julian was now having the last laugh. Mrs. Baxter fell asleep smiling. "Momma always knows best" she said to herself.

Andrew Baxter could not stop the shock and amazement from showing on his face as he read the email from his wife. The email stated that Julian's High School team had become State Champions. Julian was named MVP. He had scored 38 points, had 15 rebounds, 6 blocked shots, 5 steals and 11 assists. How do you like those numbers Mr. Baxter? His wife sarcastically added she was talking about Julian "the baby son" not Randall and a smiley face. Mr. Baxter wanted to text her back; but he stopped and started laughing. He finally collected himself and his thoughts and wrote back. "Great News Honey now we do not have to take money out of our 401K funds". He recalled his earlier statement when his wife had told him that Julian was getting better at basketball.

Mr. Baxter had thought that his wife was joking and now he knew without a doubt that Julian had what it takes to play College and possibly NBA basketball. He was named MVP twice in less than 6 months. Now he was heading to College on a full ride.

Mr. Baxter figured his best bet was to send his wife a gift. He remembered her ring finger size and figured her other hand finger should be about the same. He went to Shane's online store and ordered her a diamond ring. He had them engrave inside the ring "Love Forever & Always" and had it sent to her with a note - "...To the smartest person in the Baxter family...". Mr. Andrew Baxter hoped that his gift would make peace between him and his wife. But he knew better. She was going to tease him forever for being wrong about Julian. Mr. Baxter knew he had found a jewel when he met Angela Baxter. He was glad that he had moved quickly to lock her down before she became famous in High School, College and the WNBA.

When Mrs. Baxter tore up her knee Mr. Baxter secured approval to work from home to take care of Mrs. Baxter. He helped her to get everywhere. He took her to Doctor Appointments. He gave her piggy-back rides when she was tired of her crutches or the wheel-chair. Andrew Baxter Loved Angela when he met, and he still loved her the same way now. He smiled as he thought of the times when he had had to carry her to and from places. Mr. Baxter said that was all part of the "for better or worse program" in marriage. Now things were going to really "heat up" in the Baxter family household.

Julian has suddenly won two MVP awards and is showing out in the basketball world. Michael Jordan has his number and is calling him. He already has a full scholarship to the University of Miami that he has accepted. Randall has been a star in football for a while and is great at the game. He has not received any college scholarship offers. Mr. Baxter's world was now turning on its ear. The one child he thought would get a college scholarship has not. The other child that he thought he would have to pay for to go to college has gotten a fully paid and guaranteed scholarship.

Randall Baxter was one of the happiest people in the world for his baby brother Julian. He encouraged him to keep working on his game and the NBA would soon be his employer. Randall smiled and wondered how Samantha White and Ron Highland were taking the news about Julian. Randall hoped that they "choked" on all the good fortune that Julian was receiving. He knew that there was a lot more good fortune in store for Julian as he would be the centerpiece of the new Miami Hurricane Basketball team. Randall knew that once Julian took off and dunked on anyone; they would all know that he was "the real deal". Randall also knew he needed to get in gear for college. Right now, he had no scholarship offers. He needed to figure out his next move. What would it take to walk-on at Florida State or if not at the University of Florida football team? Randall knew he needed to figure out the costs for him to attend for at least two semesters and then earn a scholarship.

Mrs. Baxter, Pablo and Rachel were getting hit with orders on top of orders of the Hammer Dunk near the end of the game and the cup and spin dunk move to avoid the player near the end of the first half. T-shirt orders were coming in constantly. They donated to the charity for Homeless women and children, the Red Cross and programs that fed children who were not able to feed themselves. Must Ministries for the homeless and Hosea feed the Homeless received a check from the Julian Baxter Foundation. It was working. Rachel, Pablo, Mrs. Baxter and the three office assistants began to get more traction as Julian spoke about the Program and the goals of the Non-Profit Foundation. Julian said he wanted to use his story and his life to encourage and uplift others. He gave the web site information out and little cards with the name, phone, email and goals on the back.

Julian stressed to everyone that all the money donated goes to the Foundation operations costs and to various charitable organizations; Red Cross, Abused Women, Homeless women and their children, Must Ministries and Hosea Feed the homeless. He said the team is actively investigating two charities that work with youth and kids with after school programs and summer camps. He said none of it goes to him or his family.

Julian stated at one of his appearances that a teacher reminded him that to "to whom much is given; from him much is expected" and he was starting now with the Non-Profit Foundation. Julian completed his exams and registered to enter the University of Miami.

"...Most Valuable Player..."

Mrs. Baxter, Rachel, Pablo and a group of neighbors all made the ride with Julian to enter the University of Miami. There were lots of schoolmates and fans on the trip as well. Julian signed his papers and was shown his dorm room. Team Baxter helped him get settled in. Then it was off to the souvenir store.

Each member of the team was given a Hurricane Jersey to wear in support of Julian. There were hugs all around as most of Team Baxter left the Coral Gables campus to head back to Marietta. Rachel, Pablo and Mrs. Baxter stayed overnight to leave on Sunday. They headed to a nearby Holiday Inn and got two rooms. One for Mrs. Baxter and Rachel and the other for Pablo. Mrs. Baxter, Julian, Rachel and Pablo headed to the store for furnishings to add to Julian's room. Curtains, shower curtains, pillows, sheets, comforters, towels, face cloths, rugs, cutlery, coffee maker, teapot, cups, glasses, saucers, plates, salt and pepper shakers, placemats, coasters, bathrobe, jeans, t-shirts, extra sweat pants, a new laptop, a workstation for the room, printer, mop, broom, dust pan, bucket, garbage cans of assorted sizes, stapler, three-hole punch, scotch tape, assorted rulers, butter holder, spatulas, frying pan and microwave. Pablo and Mrs. Baxter had measured the bedroom for Julian. At the furniture store they gave the Manager of the store Julian's bedroom measurements. A bed that would fit Julian was ordered along with a couch and a dining table set. A coffee table set, a bookcase, a display case that would hold the TV Julian had brought from home was also ordered and paid for.

The furniture store promised they would deliver the items Sunday afternoon and set them up. Mrs. Baxter made sure that the store had the correct address for Julian and his cell phone number.

The team headed to the Office Max Store and secured a new bag for Julian to carry his laptop and notepad in. Mrs. Baxter bought Julian a set of Montblanc pens (ball point and roller ball). She also purchased a box of 24 ENERGEL rolling ball pens. She said the Montblanc set is for special events and the other pens are for everyday usage. They also ordered a set of business cards with Julian's name and in brackets and quotation marks "The Mystery Dunker". On the back of the cards was information on the Julian Baxter Foundation.

Mrs. Baxter purchased a business card case with the letter "J" in script on it for him to put the cards in when they came. Julian, Rachel, Pablo and Mrs. Baxter headed to dinner and talked about life. They also talked about the processes to update the web site and other materials. Rachel and Pablo had all the organization programs in order. They had already connected with the University of Miami films department. It was agreed that the web site would update weekly. Any thoughts or blog ideas need to be emailed to the duo at the new office by Wednesday midday or it would have to go on the next week's revisions and changes. All four of them agreed. Mrs. Baxter was acting as an unpaid Consultant to the organization.

Julian put on his newly purchased University of Miami t-shirt and they asked a server to take several group shots for them. Julian thanked the server with a $10 tip and then they took individual shots of each other.

Soon it was time to eat. Even though it was night-time Julian wanted a stack of pancakes. The server was able to get Julian "his pancakes" and they all ate heartily. Julian received a call that Brian would be arriving late Sunday afternoon and would track him down. Julian told team Baxter that he and Brian had met at the basketball camp. They had played well together and planned to play together at the "U". The team wished them both success in their careers. Then it was time to part. Mrs. Baxter and Rachel cried "tears of joy" at the success Julian was having. Julian's Mom gave him a package to open after they had left the next morning. Julian wanted to open it for all to see but she told him that it was very personal; and he needed to open it the next day in his room after they had left. Mrs. Baxter said a prayer over everyone after they had eaten and headed back to Julian's room. They dumped all the stuff that they bought in the living room. Julian would have to sleep on the floor for one night.

According to Mrs. Baxter it would not kill him. Pablo and Rachel burst out laughing along with Mrs. Baxter at the expression from Julian. "Stay humble" Mrs. Baxter reminded Julian. She gave him the present to open the next afternoon. They all gathered in a circle and said a prayer of safekeeping and good health for Julian, themselves and their friends and family. Then it was time to leave Julian. There was a group hug and Julian walked outside to watch them drive away. Rachel came back to give Julian an extra hug and kiss on the cheek. She reminded him to stay true to himself no matter what. Mrs. Baxter and the group would leave the Holiday Inn early in the morning to head back to Marietta, Georgia. Julian watched them drive away until Pablo's Black Dodge Charger faded from view.

Julian was starting a new chapter in his life. He walked back upstairs to his room and collect himself. He had a beach chair they had bought for the patio area for him. He unpacked it and put a few sheets over it. He would sleep there for the night. No floor for him Julian said to himself. He plugged in his TV and connected it. He took the supplies out of the boxes and stacked the boxes so that he could place the TV on it. He powered up the TV. He went in search of the package that his Mom had told him not to open until the next day. Julian placed the package from his mother on top of the fridge so that he would not bother it.

Julian already had a desk to study at in the Apartment. He began to clean and organize it. He put his Computer work-station on top of the desk and began to set it up. An hour later the Computer was loading the Programs and the WIFI printer was good to go. The rulers, pens, note paper, files, printing paper, file folders, file holders and other materials were set up. Julian grabbed his laptop and set it up on the desk. He had forgotten about the desk and executive chair that went with it. If he was not comfortable sleeping in the beach chair; he would sleep in the office chair. Besides it was warmer in the office area. He moved the beach chair in there.

Julian went to the bathroom and decided it was going to need "a good cleaning" before he put up the shower curtain, put in the non-slip mat and got everything set up. He sprayed bleach and 409 heavy duty bathroom cleaner in the tub, basin and toilet areas. He grabbed the bucket and a pair of rubber gloves. It was time to get to work.

Julian also got some sponges and cleaning cloths. He half-filled the bucket with water and went to work. First, he cleaned the shower area and then rinsed it off. Next, Julian cleaned the tub out and finally he cleaned out the toilet bowel. He placed the toilet bowl cleaner which would run through it with every flush of the toilet inside the bowl area. Julian placed a bowl of potpourri in a corner of the bathroom counter.

Julian put up the new shower curtain. He placed the non-slip mat in the tub. He put down the bathroom rugs. He sprayed the entire room with Lysol and closed the bathroom door. Next Julian hung up his jeans and placed his shirts, sweatshirts and other materials overhead in the closet until his furniture arrived. Next, he turned his attention to the kitchen. He unpacked a new set of silver knives, forks and spoons. He cleaned out all the drawers in the kitchen. He placed plastic mats at the bottom of each drawer. He put in the silverware trays; then he loaded them up with the cutlery and other kitchen supplies. He cleaned the cupboards in the kitchen and made a list of the necessary supplies. He made sure the dishwasher was clean. The Microwave would arrive with the other furniture tomorrow. Julian grabs his room key and wallet. He heads to the lobby area to get a couple of Pepsi sodas and some chips. He notes that the machines will also take credit cards. How convenient he says as he heads back to the second floor with his sodas, a Kit-Kat chocolate bar and chips. Julian reflects on how far he has climbed as he enters his room and locks the door behind him. He is now a member of the Miami Hurricanes basketball team. Julian knows that there will be an even bigger bullseye on him now.

Starting Monday Julian would get organized and resume his training schedule with more weight training involved. He knows that the games will involve more physical contact now. Julian puts two sheets on the beach chair and settles in with a rolled-up sheet for a pillow. The room temperature is cold; so he covers up with a comforter. He tilts back and quickly falls asleep. Julian figured he would sleep until the furniture people arrived and then sleep some more. Julian is woken up by someone banging on his door. It is the furniture people. They say they had been banging for ten to fifteen minutes. Julian apologizes and lets them in. He shows them where the bed goes, the couch, the dresser with the mirror, the bookcase and the TV Stand. The men do not waste a moment. They start bringing in stuff and quickly setting it up. The delivery men take all the boxes and packaging materials back out with them.

Soon Julian's apartment looks like a brand-new place. The men set up the bed and also bring in the large microwave unit. Once everything is in place the men ask Julian to go through the rooms and see if he wants anything changed. Julian goes on a walk through with the men and the place is setup great. There are four men. Julian gives each of them $20 as he knows what they do is really hard work. He thanks them for their work and sends them on their way. Julian now has a real bed to lie in. He checks it out. He takes the plastic off the bed and begins to make it up. The fitted sheets and then the regular sheets followed by the comforter. Next, Julian sets up the pillows and he crawls into bed to sleep for a while. He realizes that he needs an alarm clock for practices and classes. He makes a note to order one asap or go pick one up.

Julian realizes that he has to get to know the area where he lives and what is close by. He also realizes that he needs some form of transportation. Julian makes a note to check on the Uber and Lyft services in his area. Julian also makes a mental note to speak with the school staff about a place where he could get a good used car for a reasonable price. Julian wants a reliable place so that if he has any he will look at car dealers based on his new zip code when he does. No two-door cars for him; he will get a four-door Charger like Pablo's car in Silver. No black car for Julian in this Florida heat. Julian fades out as he recalls how his tears of pain have now become tears of joy. He decides he will continue his mission of speaking with youth and women's groups. He recalls that he was the man at the end of the bench last year. He savors the fact that his team won the state championship. Julian recalls what Randall and Brian had told him. There are many more moments of success ahead if he stays on the path that he is on. In his mind's eye Julian remembers that he must get a DVD player just to play the DVD's that his mother got for him to study the great players of the NBA. He has to find a Best Buy or Walmart store for the DVD Player. Julian figures he probably should go to the Walmart Store so that he can get the alarm clock and DVD Player in one place. Oh well, he thinks as he drifts off; Alarm Clock, DVD Player and Car are the order of the day. While Julian gets his first taste of sleep in his new bed Mrs. Baxter, Rachel and Pablo are on the way back to Marietta, GA. They had just eaten at a subway and are making good time. The traffic is light.

Pablo started out driving and then Rachel took over. They are closing in on the halfway mark for the trip. Mrs. Baxter wants to call Julian but the other two are telling her wait for him to call or call when she has arrived home to let him know that she was safely back home. Reluctantly, Mrs. Baxter agrees.

Brian and his family arrive on campus he quickly finds his place one building over from Julian's apartment. He and his family put his furniture and belongings together. They find a store and stock up Brian's refrigerator and cabinets with food. Lots of Pizza for the growing man. They have heard over and over about Julian and have never met him. After setting up Brian's main furniture they head over to Julian's place. After knocking a while Brian calls him on the phone. He hears stumbling around in the apartment and then the door opens. It is a half-asleep Julian mumbling about more furniture. Brian shakes him fully awake. They hug and shake hands. Julian and Brian both get a good laugh over it as does Brian's mother, father, sister, younger brother and cousin. Julian invites everyone in. Julian says as my first guests you get to break in the couch and all the other furniture.

Julian tells them he and his family arrived late yesterday and put the place together. The furniture arrived today. The delivery people left a few hours ago and I jumped in the bed. Last night I slept in a beach chair. Brian introduces his family to Julian; Beatrice his mother, Patrick his father, Diana his sister, Trevor his brother and Clyde his cousin.

The Williams family tell Julian they have heard a lot about him, and it is good to finally meet him. Julian say's now I am going to be blushing because he told you all my secrets. Brian's mother tells Julian that Brian told them how inspiring you were to him. You were the end of the bench guy on your team last year. This year a starter and MVP at the State Championship. Mr. Williams asked Julian what caused the change from bench jockey to star athlete. Brian starts to say he had it inside all the time but Julian cuts him short.

Julian tells Brian it is ok for your family to know what happened. Besides it's on the internet now. Julian tells Mr. Williams he caught his girlfriend of two years in high school cheating during the dance last year. I walked 20-plus miles home in tears. During the walk home I figured I needed to change; but change what? When I got home and looked out the window into our backyard; I saw my means to revenge.

No, I would not get violent with Samantha my ex or Ron the guy I saw her with. No, I would get better and become violent with the rim. Every time I rise to dunk; I see their faces in the rim and I want to tear them down. Mrs. Williams said that still does not explain how you got better as a player. Julian told Mrs. Williams that he began looking to past greats in the NBA for inspiration and for lessons. I studied them daily. (I still do.) I trained twice a day leading up to camp. I bought the vertical shoes to increase my vertical. I jumped rope and shot and shot and shot Free throws, jumpers and lay ups. I practiced every day; rain or shine. Each day I tried to improve in one area or another.

Gradually I improved. I began to get better at dribbling, shooting, moving and my vertical increased. Then at camp I learned a lot and improved some more. Then came "the Mystery Dunker thing" and now Michael Jordan knows my name. Brian's sister Diana said with a smile that must have been a heavy dose of revenge to your ex. Julian said he did not check for that. He said his brother Randall showed him some of the videos with people chasing her out of beauty salons and stuff. But in the end; I believe that it was karma. I had been fantasizing about her for a long, long, long time. I had talked to a lot of people over time about her long before we dated for two years. Then I caught her cheating on me; but she did not know that I had seen them. I avoided them. I went to the basketball camp and it all lit a fire under me. Now I want to make the NBA in a year's time. Diana said you have a timetable for everything. Julian responded, "now I do". Mrs. Williams chimed in that from what she has seen; and Brian has told us you are well on your way. Now watch out for those "gold-digging vixens" that will come after you here in College and in the Pros. Mrs. Williams told Julian to find himself a good hard-working female to marry and have babies with. Julian and the whole family started laughing.

Clyde chimed in that he was a PI and if he needed anyone checked out to give him a call. He gave Julian his business card. Julian shook his hand and said he certainly would. Mr. Williams said he and the family were headed back home you and Brian have a great time and look out for each other. Julian raised his right hand as if taking an oath and said; "he promised".

One by one the members of the Williams family and Clyde shook Julian's hand and wished him well. The family took off and left Brian there. After they had walked them to the car and watched them go Brian asked Julian if he had a car? Julian said he was about to ask him the same thing. They both did not have a car. Oh well said Julian let's order a pizza and figure things out. Julian told Brian that his folks had promised to help him with a used car. He figured he wanted a Dodge Charger of some sort. Brian said let's see about food first and then car stuff. They agreed.

In Julian's apartment Brian and Julian checked on the phone for the nearest pizza delivery. There was a domino's delivery program nearby. They were quick. Julian told Brian that Dominos was who he had used for his neighborhood event. They called and ordered four pizzas, two six-packs of Pepsi sodas and four orders of hot wings. While they waited for the food to arrive Julian fired up his laptop and began looking at cars. The higher the mileage the lower the price of the car. The Chargers they saw ranged from $11,000 to $22,000 in the SXT model with an average of 62,000 miles on them. They saw a 2008 Dodge Charger SRT8 with the big 8-cylinder for

$16,888. Brian told Julian he did not need that much horsepower. It had less than 30,000 miles on it. Julian said he was getting a silver colored car whatever it was. Black in Florida is too hot. They both agreed on that. Then Brian reminded Julian that he was not planning to be in school for more than a year so the 2008 would not be that bad of a deal.

Brian and Julian scrolled back to the 2008 SRT just as the pizza guy arrived. Brian showed him in as Julian ran to get his wallet. The guy gave Julian a card and wrote a note to get Julian a discount. Julian urged the guy to give them a card for Brian too. Julian gave the delivery guy $20 and Brian gave the guy another $10.00 for his time. Brian said grace and they began to eat. Brian and Julian chatted and ate to their heart's content. After getting stuffed they moved back to the laptop and began looking at cars again. They switched to the bigger work station computer. They found a 2015 SXT that had 69,500 miles on it. It was the middle model of the Dodge Charger series. It had more power than the regular Charger but not as much as the SRT. It was being sold by Mercedes Benz of Coral Gables. It was being sold for $10,500 total. Brian told Julian if you had a cash to pay they would probably take $9,500 total. You could put a warranty on it if it did not have one for $500. You have to get insurance plus get the Triple A road service for about $110. Julian said yeah that might not be such a bad deal.

Julian received an email alert on his phone. He looked at it. The email was about a Welcome Event for players Monday afternoon at the gym. Brian said he got an alert of an email on his phone but had not looked at it. Here we go said Brian. Brian and Julian looked at a campus map and figured out how to get to the Athletic Center from their buildings. They both came to the same conclusion. With a car it would be a whole lot easier. Oh well. Julian said he would call Mercedes Benz of Coral Gables about the Silver 2015 SXT. He would see what they would take for cash and if there was a warranty left on the car. He would approach his parents about assisting him with getting a short-term loan to get an auto financed.

Julian asked Brian "deal or no deal" if I am able to talk my parents into getting the car for me will you help me take care of it and you can use it too? Brian agreed, and they shook hands on it. Julian made a note on his pad to call Mercedes Benz in the morning. There was one whole pepperoni pizza left and two packs of wings. Julian gave Brian half of the pizza, 3 Pepsi sodas and one of the packs of wings in case he got hungry later. Julian and Brian took the elevator to the lobby. Julian walked to the front of his building with Brian.

Julian watched as Brian walked over to his building. Julian went back to his room and filled out the contact form for Mercedes Benz of Coral Gables. He let them know he was very interested in purchasing the Silver SXT. He went online to State Farm and found out the cost of insurance for the SXT. There was a State Farm agency not too far away. Julian sent them a contact form with the VIN for the vehicle he was trying to buy. He received an email back asking if he was associated with Walker High School in Marietta? Julian then responded yes, he had attended Walker High School in Marietta, GA. He was now attending the "U" and needed transportation. Julian knew what the next question was going to be. Are you "the Julian Baxter they call the Mystery Dunker"? Julian started laughing as he replied to the question with "Yes I am if it will get me a discount on my auto insurance. I am also planning to get Triple A Road Service". Then a message came back with a "special quote" for the Mystery Dunker.

To compare the auto rate Julian submitted a request for a quote on the same vehicle with Allstate and Geico.

The quotes from Geico and Allstate were $220.00 and $238.00 per month for full coverage. State Farm's "Special Quote" was $169.00

per month for full coverage. They also offered a 15% discount for six months paid in full. While reviewing the quotes Julian remembered the package from his mother. He raced from the study area to the kitchen. He grabbed the package down and went back to his desk. He needed a checking and savings account set up. He googled SunTrust banks in the area of his address and found two. Julian made note of both branches in his note book. His mother had given him $300 that he had spent on Pizza and tips for the furniture guys. He had close to $110.00 left. He would deposit it in the bank. Julian opened the box his mother had given him and was greeted by a variety of boxes of different types of condoms.

There was a note with the condoms that said, "protect yourself and your future; wear one every time". Love Family. Then there was a card with $500.00 in cash in it and a cashier's check for $26,500.00 with his name on it and a sticky note attached to find your dream vehicle. Julian was not big on cars like his father and his brother. He figured he could save some money and get a decent ride. He immediately called Mercedes Benz of Coral Gables and left a message for them. He wanted to test drive the SXT that he had contacted them about early in the morning. He needed a ride to the dealership. He gave his name, phone number and address. Julian folded up the cashier's check and put it in his wallet. He put the other money in his travel bag notebook except for $100 that he put in a drawer in the office desk. Julian pulled down a pair of jeans, t-shirt, cap and hoodie. He put his sneakers with his outfit along with socks and underwear.

Julian would get the car dealership to drive him to the bank to deposit the check or they could take out for the car right now and give him the change. He figured if he played his cards right; he could get the car and get the accounts set up in a few hours. After that he would then square the insurance away. He emailed the State Farm guy that if he purchased that vehicle; he would stop by with cash to pay for six months in advance. He printed out the quotation. Julian also printed out the spec sheet on the Silver SXT.

Early the next morning Julian called his Mom and told her he loved her and the family for their "protective thoughts and considerations". He also expressed his appreciation of the money and he is getting his books with the cash later today. Right now, he is on the run to get a used car. His mother reminded him not to get one that is too fancy or a car that is too expensive to maintain. He promised his Mother that he would make her proud. Julian told his Mom that he loved her.

Julian quickly called the dealership to speak with the Sales Manager. He was put on hold and then a man came on the line and introduced himself as John Reese. He told Julian he was the Sales Manager at the dealership. Julian gave his name and address. He said he had a few issues; the car that I called and emailed you about is it available? If I paid you cash how much would you take for it? Does it have a warranty or not? Mr. Reese said to Julian; to answer your questions the car is available. If you paid cash for it, we would take $910.00 off by cash or cashier's check.

Mr. Reese told Julian that the vehicle has some warranty left on it. However, as you are joining UM's basketball team, we would give you a full warranty free of charge for 18,000 miles from today. Julian explained his dilemma. He had a cashier's check in his name from his parents that he had to pay some other things with. How can we work it out? Mr. Reese said if you deposit it; you will have the funds in 48 hours. Put $100.00 down cash and we would give you a temp purchase agreement. We would process the final paperwork when you come back with the cashier's check or cash.

Mr. Reese said his store would give coverage for the vehicle for the week and have it cleaned and filled with gas by the time he got there. Mr. Reese asked Julian if that was good enough for him? Julian said he could live with that program. Mr. Reese said he was sending a car with a gentleman named Leon McKenzie to pick Julian up. He will be driving my car said Mr. Reese. It is a Black Dodge Challenger SRT. Julian said he would be waiting outside the building. He would sign the temp purchase paperwork and leave to get his bank accounts set up. Julian hung up.

Julian tossed his print outs of the car info, insurance and other papers into his travel bag. He made sure that he had the correct address of the SunTrust bank near the school. He caught a quick shower and dressed. Julian made sure he had his phone, ID and other info before he closed the door to his apartment and headed down in the elevator. Julian called Brian to make sure that his family was fine.

Julian told Brian that his family were a funny and fun-filled bunch especially your Mom. She does not play. She is direct and right to the point. Brian told Julian now you know why I act the way that I do. They both laughed. Brian asked Julian where he was. Julian said he was off to the bank to set up a checking acct. He would explain when he saw him at the welcome event.

Julian wanted to surprise Brian. As he waited for the ride to the dealership Julian realized he had not eaten. He would need to stop by McDonalds and get some pancakes. First things first though; he needed to have transportation. The University of Miami campus was a whole lot bigger than Walker High School. It probably could hold 15 Walker High School locations on the campus of the "U". Julian made a note in his notebook to get Pablo, Rachel, Mom, Dad, Randall basketball jerseys with his number on them when they came out. A short time later a black fully loaded Dodge Challenger turned the corner and headed towards his building. Julian instinctively knew that this was his ride. He started waving. The driver pulled up and lowered the window and asked if he was Julian Baxter. Julian said he was and raced around the car to get in. Time was a factor. He needed to get the car matter and bank matter completed ASAP so that he could get some rest and be ready for the University of Miami welcome meeting.

Julian introduced himself to Leon. He asked Leon if there was a McDonalds restaurant on the way to the dealership. Leon told him yes.

Julian asked Leon if they could stop quickly to get some food. He had not eaten at all since early last night. Leon nodded that he understood how that could be. He stressed that Mr. Reese was waiting and probably was timing him. Julian laughed and said he understood that and would take the full blame. They raced to a McDonalds about ten miles away. Julian asked Leon if he wanted anything "his treat". Leon said no. Julian ordered a large coffee, creamers, sugar, scrambled eggs, double order of hot cakes and sausages. He paid for the food and fidgeted as the clock ticked off more time. One of the servers asked him his name. He told Julian that he looked like the guy in that "Mystery Dunker" video. The guy said the "Mystery Dunker" was reportedly enrolling in the University of Miami. Julian smiled and said nothing. He received his order, got extra napkins and various condiments and then he gave the guy that asked who he was a $10 handshake and said yes that was him. He was now at the "U".

Julian raced to the car before the man could tell his friends and other customers. Julian hopped in the car and told Leon to hurry and leave. Leon took him at his word and sped out of the McDonalds parking lot just as people streamed out of the store shouting out "welcome to Miami Mystery Dunker". Leon started laughing as they headed to the express way. He told Julian they should be at the dealership within 15/20 minutes. So, you're "that guy" he told

Julian. Leon said he had seen the story in the Magazines and on the internet about Julian.

Leon told Julian you had a run of bad luck for a while but it's now "All Golden for you". Julian said yeah that was a different way of looking at it. Leon told Julian he had read how Julian had been the guy at the end of the bench getting no run on his basketball team. He had also read how Julian had caught his girl cheating and said nothing. Leon said you became like Batman; in the lab tinkering and working on things. Then you came out as the Mystery Dunker and won the first MVP and now here you are on top of the world.

Julian told Leon; truth be told after the issue with Samantha instead of beating Ron up or getting into a confrontation I used basketball as my outlet. Every time I rise to dunk on someone; I imagine they are Samantha and Ron. It gives me more power and more energy to ram that basketball home. I saw a guy in my research on the basketball greats and I patterned my game after him; Shawn Kemp. Shawn Kemp was 6' 10" and played for 15 years. He was able to handle the ball and went over the top of everyone on his way to the rim. My "The Hammer" dunk is based on Shawn Kemp, MJ and Dominique Wilkins. Oh, said Leon; that is where that dunk came from.

Yeah; Julian told Leon "the Hammer dunk" is a combination of three dunks. MJ and Dr. J's foul line dunk, Shawn Kemp's two hand power dunk and Dominique's power dunk. Soon they were at the Mercedes Benz of Coral Gables dealership. Leon rushed Julian in to meet with Mr. John Reese. Julian shook Mr. Reese's hand and then asked Leon if he had a business card. When Leon gave him a business card Julian gave him $20 for lunch.

Mr. Reese told Julian to leave his food and materials in his office for a brief second and then he would give him time to eat. Mr. Reese walked Julian to the back of the showroom and pulled the covers off a 2014 Silver SRT8 that the dealership was giving Julian for the same price as the SXT.

Mr. Reese told Julian that the dealer ship was going to "eat the difference in price". We do not want the "Mystery Dunker of the University of Miami" riding around town without power. Mr. Reese told Julian to pick his chin up off the floor. Julian was standing there staring blankly with his mouth wide open. He asked Mr. Reese twice if "This was the car he was getting". The company would write the other costs off as Marketing expenses. Mr. Reese told Julian to get behind the wheel. Julian was grinning from ear to ear. Mr. Reese told Julian to start her up and pull out in front of the showroom. Leon and the staff had already opened the main showroom door so that Julian could ride out. Mr. Reese said he just wanted to take a photo handing the keys off to Julian just as they had with other customers. He pointed to a wall of customers and their photos. Julian and Mr. Reese took their photos and then all the staff on shift gathered around the car and had a banner that read "Welcome to Miami Mystery Dunker" – Mercedes Benz of Coral Gables. Mr. Reese told Julian to keep the keys. He had two more sets for him in the office. Julian and Mr. Reese raced to Mr. Reese's office. Julian was given a side table to eat on. Mr. Reese prepared the temp purchase papers and got a copy of Julian's driver's license.

Mr. Reese gave Julian two copies of the insurance information covering the car and anyone he let drive it. He suggested Julian keep one in the glove compartment. Mr. Reese also handed Julian a typed document that was being sent to the Licensing department to get special tags for Julian. His tag would read – "M DUNKR1". Mr. Reese made two copies of that document as well. Julian showed Mr. Reese the cashier's check from his parents. Mr. Reese said the funds should be in his account by Wednesday. Mr. Reese the sales Manager at Mercedes Benz of Coral Gables told Julian he could come in next weekend and get the proper paperwork done. He said whichever is convenient to him he was ok to do.

Mr. Reese told Julian yes, he could come in sooner but to be safe he was authorizing full coverage for the car until next weekend. He told Julian the temporary tag that was being put on his car would cover 90 days because when you order customized tags; they have to search nationwide for anyone having a similar one. He had Julian sign a temporary purchase order document. He made two copies of it and gave them to Julian. He was all set. A temporary tag was already placed on his car and it had a plastic cover over it so it would not tear or get wet.

Julian thanked Mr. Reese for his help and the "special deal". He told Mr. Reese that he was scared the auto purchase was going to be complicated and a major ordeal.

Mr. Reese told Julian we try to take care of all our customers but the earnestness and efforts that you made in contacting us spoke volumes about you. Then when my son told me about the Mystery dunker story; and I read it I immediately contacted the GM and we put together this deal for you. Mr. Reese told Julian that you have seen the car I drive it has the same engine as your own. The car you are getting is fast. When the windows are up you will not realize how fast you are going. Mr. Reese told Julian to make sure to check your speed constantly. Mr. Reese also cautioned Julian to take it easy. Do not rush to drive fast. Get to know the car before you do. Mr. Reese gave Julian three business cards with his cell phone number on the back. One is for you to give to a friend. One is for you to keep in your wallet and the other is to stay at home. He told Julian the car has only 48,000 miles. You have a full warranty and free oil changes as long as you own the car. He told Julian to call him if he has any issues at all with the car. Mr. Reese gave him the business card of a personal friend that will come by to clean and detail the car for you at half price. Julian told Mr. Reese thanks for everything.

Julian and Mr. Reese shook hands and Mr. Reese made sure that Julian put all the papers in his brief bag. Then Julian asked Mr. Reese if there was anything that he could do for him since he had done so much for him. Mr. Reese grabbed several Mercedes Benz of Coral Gables T-shirts and two basketballs for Julian to sign. He signed them and shook hands with Mr. Reese. The staff came up requesting autographs.

Julian obliged all of them. After he had signed everything he jumped into the Charger and headed to the SunTrust bank. He had already printed out the directions. At the bank Julian waited to speak with Mr. Trent Broom the branch Manager. After a twenty-minute wait Julian was ushered into the office of Mr. Broom. Julian explained his dilemma. He showed Mr. Broom the cashier's check and the need to get a car. The cashier's check was a Georgia check and it should clear immediately. He promised Julian the funds would be in his checking account on Wednesday morning. He asked Julian if he wanted all of it to go to a checking account? Julian said for the moment yes. He needed to open a checking and savings account right away.

Mr. Broom took $100 from Julian to open the savings account and he used the cashier's check for the opening deposit of the checking account. Mr. Broom suggested that Julian open a Roth IRA later on after he gets settled. He advised Julian that while he would be saving for his future expenditures and retirement he could withdraw from it in an emergency situation. He also recommended that Julian take a closer look at the stock market and find a good broker. Mr. Broom said he strongly recommended Morgan Stanley and a couple other Individual brokers. He gave Julian all their numbers plus the number for the stock broker department at SunTrust Bank.

Mr. Broom reminded Julian of the Laws of Compound Interest. Mr. Broom told Julian that he should read up on Warren Buffet and "the advantage of compound interest". Mr. Broom stated that Julian had youth working in his favor. Mr. Broom urged Julian to "take advantage of his youth". He also gave Julian a debit card for the accounts. Mr. Broom promised a new card would be in the mail to him in a few weeks but the one he was giving him would allow him to access his accounts immediately. They set up a pin for the card.

Mr. Broom told Julian that the longer he let his investments or savings simmer the better it would be for him in the long run. Mr. Broom thanked Julian for his new accounts and gave him a business card for him and one for a friend with his private cell phone number on the back. They shook hands and Julian headed back to the "U" campus.

Julian saw a music store sign ahead. He pulled in and bought a few CD's to listen to; George Benson, Mary J, Luther Vandross, Sounds of

Blackness, Teddy Riley & the Winans, New Edition, Anita Baker, Mary Mary, Chante Moore, Johnny Gill, Tyrese, Najee, Sade, the soundtrack from New Jack City and he headed out. He had two of Najee, Sounds of Blackness, Mary Mary, Sade and Tyrese. One set was for the apartment. It was closing in on 12:30pm. The Welcome meeting was set for 3:30pm in the Athletic Center. Julian saw a Walgreens store. He needed two alarm clocks. He got an electric one that had a slot for batteries as a backup. He got the clock and he purchased another smaller clock that was totally on batteries. Julian purchased an extra package of batteries for both clocks. Julian also saw that the store had auto supplies. He purchased an Executive Club anti-theft bar that was placed across the steering wheel and locked. Usually thieves would leave cars with the Club behind and go steal the one with no club. Julian figured he would head to the Apartment and catch a nap. He pulled up to his building and parked where his vehicle was constantly visible. He took the Club device out of the packaging and put it on the steering wheel. He locked the Club device into place.

Julian figured after a while he needed to get the car tinted also. Right after he got into his apartment; he pulled out a t-shirt, underwear and socks to change into for the Welcome meeting.

Julian pulled out the paperwork for the car and called the State Farm office and asked for a revised quote. He gave them the new VIN number. A short time later the quote came over and Julian said he had no problem with it. The rate had gone up to $189.50 per month. He would still get a 15% discount if he paid for 6 months in advance. Julian let the State Farm office know that he would be coming by Wednesday or Thursday to activate the Policy. Julian then called Triple A and ordered Gold coverage for his vehicle. It was now $140.00 for the year. He ordered it online. Triple A gave him a temp card to print out and use if he needed to. Julian printed out several copies and marked one for the glove compartment. A proper card would be coming in the mail. He put one in his shoulder bag and cut one down and placed it in his wallet. Julian called Brian and told him to call him at just about 2:45pm. He had been busy and needed a nap before the meeting. Julian said he and Brian could ride together to the event. Brian figured he meant Uber, Lyft or one of the car services on campus and thought nothing of it. Both men caught a quick nap before heading to the meeting. Julian was laughing as he slept. He could not wait to see Brian's face when he pulled up in his new car???

Julian went to sleep and soon it was time to get up. The alarm clock went off and then Brian called.

Julian said he was catching a quick shower. He told Brian they could call for a ride from his building to the Athletic Center. Brian said he would meet Julian out front of his building. Julian said ok and that he was heading to the shower now to freshen up. Julian quickly dressed and grabbed his shoulder bag. He put a couple extra pads of paper in the bag and some extra pens. He put on his black hoodie, black jeans, sneakers, socks, underwear and fresh t-shirt. Julian made sure that he had his keys, phone and wallet with him. Julian headed downstairs and powered up the "Silver Bullet".

Julian pulled over to the side of Brian's building out of sight. He waited for Brian to call him and ask him where he was? Julian did not answer his text message; he drove around the corner and stopped in front of Brian and rolled the window down "do you need a ride Sir?" he asked. Brian started hollering, screaming and jumping all over the place. He kept asking Julian if this was "his ride"? Julian finally told him to stop circling the car and get in or they would be late for the event. Brian hopped in the car and put his seatbelt on. He kept saying "wow, wow, wow" the whole ride to the Athletic Center. Once there Julian parked and put the Club device back in place. He grabbed Brian by the arm; come on we cannot start out being late. They raced inside and met Coach Terry Hall, Drew Basden the Athletic Director and Ms. Yvonne Marshall, the President of the University of Miami. All three said they were glad to meet the "Mystery Dunker" and his partner in crime. Julian told them all that for the record on off days and non-playing weekends he would like to organize or be a part of any University of Miami Community related events.

Julian told the group that he would do all he could to assist the University of Miami win games on the court and be a goodwill ambassador off the court. He also believed in supporting other teams. Where possible he would be attending other teams' sporting events. The President of the School and the AD both gave Julian and Brian business cards. They told Brian and Julian to call them if they needed help with anything. Both men promised to keep in touch with them. Julian made a mental note to get 6 different Thank You cards. One each for the AD, President and the Coach. One from Brian and one from him.

There were a number of players from last year's team along with other recruits there. Julian and Brian went over and introduced themselves to everyone. A DJ was spinning tunes, there was food off to one side. There were cheerleaders and a section for the team fans and Alumni to gather. Julian and Brian walked to the center of the court and looked at each other and hi-fived each other. The thing they had talked about doing was now a reality. It was now their reality. As they looked around the 9,500-seat arena they thought about the different environments. Both realized that with a full house; the fans would give them far more energy than the 1 to 3 thousand seat gyms they had previously played in. "This is going to be fun" Brian and Julian said at the same time. Brian told Julian he could imagine the noise and stuff when he drops "The Hammer" in the first game. They were both wide-eyed with excitement and anticipation. Both men knew that they were going to have to work even harder than they did in High School to succeed at this level.

In College there are always lots of good players and in order to get an edge they were going to have to get in tip-top shape physically. Both of them had to stay mentally sharp and watch lots of film of their opponents. Brian and Julian made the commitment to do just as they did at camp. They could care less about parties and stuff. They wanted to be the best that they could be. They were on a mission. They would spend their spare time studying film and game plans.

It is said the game of basketball is played at one speed in High School and it speeds up with every level up you go. Now the two men would have to fight harder for rebounds. They also had to be better dribblers or risk having their balls stolen constantly. They had to improve their shooting and especially their Free throw shooting. The coaching staff was introduced and each of the returning players were introduced. A list was read of the players joining the team. Brian and Julian spent most of their time talking with the strength and conditioning coach about improving their bodies.

They both wanted to get stronger and much tougher to withstand the physical nature of the game at the college level. Assistant Coach, Jorge Espinosa promised Brian and Julian that he would make their bodies stronger and tougher without sacrificing flexibility. He told Brian and Julian that what they wanted would take continuous work and proper diet. The two of them told coach that they were on board and shook his hand. They said tomorrow we organize our classes and practice schedules and Wednesday we will get with you and begin training.

Julian, Brian and their other teammates were introduced to Miss Roslyn Martinez the lead student counsellor for athletes in the basketball program. She gave each of the men a business card. If any of them had a problem with getting a class, the class schedule or any academic matter they were to call her office at once.

The coaching staff welcomed each and every one to the campus. There was a tour of the Facilities. Each member of the team would receive a key that allows them to be in the gym at any hour of the day or night. He advised the members of the team and others involved that the entire Athletic center is under video surveillance 24/7.

He showed the group phones that are directly connected to the school Police Station, Medical Center and the Security Department. He said medical or police help would be here in minutes. There were also multiple areas with portable oxygen and defibrillators on the walls of the center

The team toured the massive weight room, sauna, whirlpool area, pool area, picnic area and patio area. Head basketball Coach, Terry Hall showed the guys and gals the new grilling area. He told them from time to time he makes his presence felt with his grilled-chicken. Coach said he also was good with barbecue ribs. Everyone gave Coach Hall a round of applause and lots of cheering. Some of the players said they can't wait to sample the ribs and chicken. The whole group broke out in laughter. After the tour there was a gathering in the main hall where the DJ was spinning tunes.

There was more food, members of the faculty, training staff members, alumni, coaches from other sports teams at "The U" and security staff. The security staff leader did mention by way of a "Special announcement" that if any of the new students had vehicles on campus they should register them with the school. He said it would be a form you fill out when you sign up for classes. The vehicle would be issued a sticker/decal for preferred parking. The new members of the team were asked to meet with the coaching staff at 11am on Thursday in the Athletic Center. After the meeting with the coaches the student/athletes they would be able to register for their classes in an area of the Athletic Center. There are also study rooms here in the Athletic center some with computers and some without. There would be people here to register you for your classes. There are morning, midday and night weight training sessions for those athletes wanting to get a head start on the practice season. Those sessions are 7:30am, 12pm and 8pm except on home game nights.

The coaching staff said all the student/athletes would be issued temp passes to get in and out of the school, gym, cafeteria and eating areas, libraries and other facilities until their proper credentials arrive at their mailboxes. Each member of the team was given a new gym bag, a backpack, a dozen t-shirts, two caps, six pairs of shorts, two sweat suits, two extra pairs of sweat pants, two pairs of sneakers, two pairs of cross trainers, two hoodies and a pair of sunglasses with the UM logo on them.

Each member of the team was also given a handbook on the University of Miami, history, personal conduct code, last year's team and plans for this year along with the new upcoming season schedule.

Julian made a note to spend time training right away. He also wanted to support the other sports that were going on until his classes started. He figured that if he showed up and supported the other sports when his time came; they would do the same for him and the men's basketball team. After the presentations and collecting the gift bags and supplies Julian and Brian headed home to their apartments in the "Silver Bullet". Better yet, to celebrate they would find a nearby restaurant and go get something to eat. They put dining places in their phones and found out that there was a Ruby Tuesday restaurant not too far away. They said goodbye to everyone and headed out in the "Silver Bullet". Brian was busy taking photos and posting them on twitter and Instagram to his accounts. He had taken photos of the event, the other players and staff. He took photos of the "Silver Bullet" and of them riding along. Julian told Brian he needed to concentrate on where he was going; to settle down.

A short time later they found the restaurant and were very quickly seated near the back. TV's were blaring sports and news. They had the server change their TV to sports. Brian and Julian watched stories about the World Cup, the NBA (Kawhi Leonard, Carmello Anthony, LeBron James, Dwayne Wade and others) and which team were they all going to.

There were stories about TO and Julian said TO was his hero in that he wanted to be the total opposite of him. He and Brian debated whether or not TO should have gotten into the Hall of Fame. Then came news that Kawhi Leonard was being sent to the Toronto Raptors in exchange for DeMar Rozan and another player. Now the NBA world waits to see what LeBron James and the Lakers along with Kawhi Leonard and the Raptors do in the upcoming year. In the NFL there is all the talk about the NFL players kneeling during the playing of the National Anthem.

Julian gave Brian a set of keys to the car. He advised him that once the insurance from State Farm was in place; he would be able to drive the car at any time. Right now, they were riding on the insurance coverage of the Mercedes Benz of Coral Gables Dealership. Brian could not drive this week. Julian explained that his parents had sent him a gift to get the car and he had set up an account where the funds would be available Wednesday. He would go to the bank and then the dealership to pay for everything and the car would be his. The two had a good time at the restaurant. They ordered baked chicken breasts, brown rice, baked potatoes, salad with French and Italian dressing, orange juice and ice cream for desert. They ate, joked around and Brian really cracked up when Julian told him the license plate that Mr. Reece had ordered for him. Brian told "Julian now he truly was a mini celebrity". Julian said you sound just like my Mom.

She was stressing to me to be careful what I do, what I say and who I hang out with because even when I do not see them; there are people watching me.

Brian told Julian my Mom, Dad, Uncle and Sister told me to tell you the exact same thing. Brian said my sister has advised me to be your bodyguard and run interference for you. Brian said from the short time I have known you I have seen your dedication and coolness. However, since you have won the awards and gotten the stories written about you more people know of you now. You are going to be tested in games and stuff. You also are going to be tested by "jealous people". Brian reminded Julian of the guy that was talking all the trash at the All-Star game.

Brian said you thought that guy was a "pain" wait until we are in "really big games" here at the "U". People are going to try to bait you and also bug you until you snap. Even in practice people are going to bug you. Brian told Julian to remember that usually in exchanges like that it is the person retaliating that usually gets caught. Brian told Julian that he has to know that there are some guys on the team from last year that are jealous of you. There are going to be people on your own team rooting for you to fail because of what you have accomplished in such a short space of time. Julian said he kind of thought that but he would let the coaches handle the team. Those that do give him a hard time; he will just leave them alone. Brian told him when he played football he would physically be here in the present but his mind could go anywhere he wanted it to go. Brian said he mostly ignored people.

Brian said when other players tried to get under his skin he would be like the water boy. Use their tactics against them. The trash talking would make me smile and then I would light them up. Brian said he lit up guys that talked a lot of trash with him along with their runners, receivers and quarterbacks. They both laughed. Brian said he had to lose weight after he stopped playing football. Julian said he could not imagine Brian being bigger and thicker. Brian pulled out his phone and showed him photos. They both got a good laugh out of it. Julian told Brian that he was scary looking in pads. Brian said he did not have Julian's hops; he needed to lose weight to be able to dunk.

Julian said he only wanted a bigger chest and upper body to absorb the physicality of the game at this level and in the NBA. Brian and Julian both agreed they wanted to maintain the long lean look but with a decent upper body. They agreed to start training the next day at 10am in the athletic center. They would start with their usual, free throw, shooting, jumping rope and long-distance shooting. Practice was the means to them getting better. It had worked so far, and it would work in the future. They ate, watched a little bit more sports and then headed to their apartments at the "U". They would begin their new road to being good for the "U" the next day. Right now, it was rest time. They spotted a Walmart on the way back to the apartments. They went in and purchased some toiletries and goodies. Julian made sure that they got a stack of varied Thank You cards. He gave half the stack to Brian.

The Walmart also sold stamps, so Julian bought a book for him and one for Brian. He told Brian as they headed to the car that he had to send a card to everyone he met at the meeting that was a coach or school official. If you have a problem with them let me know and I will help you. It is a short note by hand something like "It was great to meet you. I want to be an integral part of the athletic program but also the community program at "The U". It was a pleasure to meet you. Have a GREAT Day. Julian told him he could change it to how he felt but that was the essence of the message. To make sure that you do not forget it I will email it to you. Julian started laughing as Brian said "you are worse than my Sister, Mom and Dad when it comes to doing things". They cruised back to their apartments. Julian dropped Brian off and got out as Brian grabbed his stuff out of the trunk. Soon you will be driving the "Silver Bullet" Julian told Brian. Brian headed into his building and Julian headed a block down to his. He parked and put his club device in place. Julian grabbed his travel bag and goodies out of the trunk. Julian had to make a second trip to get his groceries out of the car. After Julian had gotten everything into his Apartment Julian sent Randall a photo of his new ride with the tag info the dealer had ordered for him. Julian said he was after a basic 6-cylinder car; but they gave him a "special price" on this one. He told Randall they made him an offer he could not refuse. Randall told Julian he was transferring to "The U" so that he could drive the "Silver Bullet". Randall reminded Julian that this is another of the many blessings that he was receiving.

Remember all those free tutoring lessons, free help with book reports, free help with writing papers that you did for others this is God paying you back in spades. He told his baby brother to take care of himself and to let Mom and Dad know what he got. Julian told Randall that he was sending them an email in a second. Randall told his brother that he loved him and said he was always praying for him. Julian told Randall the same. Julian emailed his Mom and Dad photos of the "Silver Bullet" and the ordered tag info.

Julian's father was happy for him and told him to be very careful and alert at all times while driving. He told Julian to remind Brian to do the same. Julian's mother was upset that he had spent all the money they had given him for the "Silver Bullet". Julian told his mother that he spent way less than she would have thought. The Sales Manager said they gave him a large discount on the car to attract attention for them by him riding around in a nice car. People would come to the dealership to try to get a deal. Julian said he is paying his insurance 6 months ahead to get a 15% discount and the banker at SunTrust is working with me to get me a money manager. Julian told his mother that Brian said Hi and he was going crazy over the car. He and I will be the only drivers of the car unless Randall transfers to "The U". Then he would be added to the list. Julian asked his mother what was the deal on the condoms? His mother said his father and her had read about all the athletes accused of rape and the father of various children by many young ladies. They did not want that to happen with him. Mrs. Baxter and Julian both began laughing.

Mrs. Baxter told Julian that she was proud of the man that he had become. She told him to go and drop "The Hammer" on someone. They both laughed and exchanged "I Love You's" and then hung up.

Julian sent emails to Rachel and Pablo. He told them that he had his first welcome meeting with the coaching staff and it went great. He said the University of Miami or "The U" is a huge campus. My parents helped me get a new ride. He sent them photos of the "Silver Bullet". He told them that he was going to need them to send him color copies of their driver's licenses so that they can be added to the insurance to drive it. (Remember; it is only a car.) He told them both that he missed them and appreciated what they were doing with the web site. Once he turned pro the web site would be totally revamped and both of them would be well-paid members of the staff. He told both of them that he loved them for life and hoped to see them soon. "Take care and Love Ya".

Julian figured he would sleep late and then get something to eat with Brian and begin their workouts. He laid out one of the sweat suits, shorts, sneakers, t-shirt, he threw a few wrist bands into his new gym bag. He put a pair of the new cross-trainers in the bag as well. He put extra t-shirts and jerseys inside the gym bag. Julian placed one of his jump ropes in the gym bag also. He put his gym bag near the front door along with his travel bag with all his documents. Julian caught a shower and put on his PJ's. Julian stepped out onto his balcony and looked out over the University of Miami campus lights. He reflected on how far he had come in a short time. There was still more to do and achieve.

Heading to the Next Level...

The University of Miami... **[...The "U"...]**

A New Chapter In Life...

Julian knew that he had gotten better as a basketball player now he had to become better as a man. He joined the Commerce Club to learn about starting and running a business. He volunteered at the local Boys & Girls club to work with the kids in his spare time. He became the big brother many of them wanted but never had. He answered the kids honestly about why he never brought a girl with him to the club like some of the other athletes. He told the kids he was working with "truthfully" his girlfriend had left him; so now he was concentrating totally on school. He wanted the University of Miami basketball team to be successful. Julian answered all their questions. He also noticed how many of them picked up the drills and insight of the game that he and other members of the University of Miami team were showing them. He told all of them that he now had a dream of going to the NBA so he had to improve his game. Julian and Brian had three weeks before school and full basketball team practices started.

Julian and Brian volunteered with other athletes for the Boys & Girls Club. They also visited the sick in the various Children's Hospitals in Miami. They also began to visit and cheer on the swimming team, softball team, baseball team, football team and the soccer teams. Brian, Julian and other members of the Basketball team made it a point to wear their basketball team shirts to let them know who they were. They hung together with the soccer team and football team players at various competitions. Brian and Julian were learning about each other as well as making new fans.

Finally, it was class time and then basketball practice time. It started with after class practice and then practicing in the morning before classes and then later after classes. Brian and Julian along with a couple other players had begun working out twice a day as long as it did not interfere with practice or class schedules.

Brian, Julian and their workout mates were gaining muscle and losing fat. Now many of them had arm muscles they could flex and show off. They needed to put in twice as much work and dedication. College was at a different level from High School. The competition was about to get tougher. Tomorrow classes and basketball practices would begin. Late that night on his balcony Julian thought about things and his future. He stared into the night and saw that the NBA was his future "IF he put in the work and dedication". He made a promise to do exactly that.

Julian made a silent promise to the night air to give his very best to the team and the community. He smiled as he closed the door and headed to bed. He knelt and said his prayers; thankful for the many blessing that had come his way after the issues with Samantha White. He crawled into bed and got ready for the next chapter in his life.

Randall lay in bed thinking of his little brother and the new chapter in his life. He smiled as he thought of the "silver bullet" ride that Julian had purchased. He knew though that his brother would have to be ready for war each and every time he stepped on the basketball court from this point on. Randall had watched the video of the state championship game with Julian. He had told Julian after watching the game that he had done all that he could to help them bring home the win. The only thing he saw that he might have changed was that Julian was being "too unselfish". Several times he could have attacked the basket a bit more. However, what more could you say; the Walker High School team had won. Julian had scrapped and tussled with everyone for every rebound. He had taken the ball to the basket hard. He had never lost his composure even when they deliberately hacked him and fouled him.

Randall knew that the seed had been planted for Julian to make it to the NBA by his neighbors, Michael Jordan, his coaches and his family. Julian had walked 20-plus miles home from the school gym after "the incident" with Samantha White. The NBA was around the corner.

Brian's father (Patrick Williams) had told him that when Julian cannot retaliate for being bullied on the court as a teammate and friend he would have to step in. Mr. Williams had told Brian to look at Charles Oakley and at the Detroit Bad Boys games. When their leaders could not afford to get a foul or payback someone for a previous foul they were the ones that gave that person a hard foul or a hard body check. His father said your team needs Julian on the floor in full flight. You have to do the maintenance and make sure that the tarmac is cleared for takeoff. His father asked him if he understood what that meant? Brian told his father he was 100% on board. Brian's sister, Diana said you have to be the bodyguard for Julian. Even if it is a teammate giving Julian a hard time you have to take his side. You are the new- comers and some of them are probably jealous of how popular Julian already is. It's just like the NBA teams and LeBron James. They all envy the fact that LeBron James is the one they talk about every time the NBA is talked about.

As Brian climbed into bed he reflected on his family's thoughts and especially his father's request that Brian be an enforcer and "body-guard" for Julian. He smiled as he recalled his sister and young brother putting their "two cents" into the matter. Brian knew that the road from here on out would be rough for both he and Julian. They were going to be tested and then tested some more. They needed to be in tip-top-shape physically and mentally.

Mrs. Baxter lay in her bed and silently prayed that her baby boy would be able to impose his will on others at the College level.

Julian had done it in the High School games and as long as he

maintained his cool he could do it at the College level. She had seen his determination in the fact that he had walked 20-plus miles home to avoid Samantha White. She had seen him practicing in the hot Georgia sun and in the rain. If he maintained that level of training and continued to develop and grow the NBA was not a dream but a reality. It was the next stop on the train of Life for Julian. Mrs. Baxter in her mind's eye imagined her child walking across the NBA stage as a first-round draft pick. She had never thought that it would be possible after Julian's freshman year at Walker High School. He had a been a streaky scorer but now he had consistency and fearlessness in his abilities. She figured as long as he does not get hurt; Julian would be making that walk across a stage as first round or at worst a second round NBA pick. She smiled as she went to sleep.

Rachel and Pablo were also silently praying for Julian as they turned in for the night. They knew he had a tough road ahead and wanted the best for him. Rachel got down on her knees and sent a few prayers that Julian would succeed. Early the next morning Julian began his previous routine. He started doing his 50 pushups, 50 sit-ups and 50 crunches. He had to ensure that his core was in top shape. Everything else would take care of itself. He made breakfast and began studying the upcoming season schedule. Half of the 16-game schedule would be played at home. Once they made the NCAA tournament they would have to travel to New York. The team had just missed making the NCAA tournament last year and had to settle for going to the NIT tournament. They were beaten in the first round by University of Minnesota. This was a new year. This was a "new beginning" that was the way Julian saw it. This year was a Job Interview for a slot in the NBA. He had to make the most of it whether his fellow team members liked him or not.

Julian made breakfast and while he ate he studied the games that were available on YouTube of the "U's" basketball games. They had two good guards. They had one good scorer from the wing but their defense was terrible. There was no "help defense" on the team. They tried full court pressure and were beaten in two passes. One pass to the half court area and the other to the basket. The other teams were beating their press coverage with layups. This was a new year and it definitely would "NOT BE ALLOWED" this year.

Julian made note of the small forward that was a scorer. His name was Paul Wood. Put him on one side at shooting guard and move Julian to Small forward and Brian at power forward. Keep the Center Maxwell Strong. He was quick and grabbed lots of rebounds. He also was able to run the floor really well. He was from Puerto Rico. He had started out playing soccer as his first love and then switched to basketball as he started to grow taller. He was now 6' 11" tall and strong. When he caught an alley oop and threw it down the whole neighborhood knew.

Julian made his notes and thoughts visible on paper. He felt that the final decisions would be made by the coaching staff. He would do all that he could to get the team to the league title or the NCAA title despite the heavy odds. The year before they had been eliminated in the first round of the NIT. Not this year! Not having it...! At minimum Julian felt that he and his team could get to the second round of the NCAA tournament this year. Anything beyond that would be gravy or icing on the cake.

"...Most Valuable Player..."

Julian knew that all of the team members were going to have to buy-in on "giving 100% for them to have a chance in the NCAA tournament. He would start at the first practice to get to know every member of the team. If they did not buy in to them getting to the NCAA tournament again then it was on them; but he would be going all out to win. He went to sleep with a smile. Have a good year at the "U" and he would be set for the NBA. Oh yeahhhhhhhhh...

As soon as his alarm went off Julian was on the move. He began his coffee maker. He then began stretching and working on his 50 crunches, 50 sit-ups and 50 pushups. After that, it was time for more stretching and then a rush to the shower and off to his first class. Then he would have a 45-minute break before his second class started. His third class would start a half hour after the second one and then it would be a short rest period and then basketball practice.

For some reason Julian was not nervous about his first basketball practice at the "U".

Julian had grown physically. He had grown mentally. He was now more familiar with different types of players and the nuances of the game. He was ready for the challenge to make an impact on the team. Julian knew he just had to play his game and do his part. He would have to trust the other team members to do their part. He looked forward to the coaching team and their plans for the year. He was ready.

The team assembled and began warming up with laps and then layup lines. The team came together in a huddle. The coach assigned different players to work with different assistant coaches for a time. Julian was put with the shooting coach and Brian was there also.

"...Most Valuable Player..."

Coach Hugh Grant introduced himself to all the team members. He had them all sign a sheet and print their names. He also had a note pad that had individual evaluation forms on the players. He had each player take three jump shots and also shoot three free throws. The players were also being filmed by a group of student interns for the team. Coach Grant evaluated the balance, follow through and mechanics of each player. Three things stood out to Coach Grant especially on the Free throw line. He stressed to all the players that the "Free throw line can win you a game or lose you a game...".

Coach Grant stressed to the players the same things that Randall had stressed to Julian. Make Free shooting the same as a dance. Each time you have to follow the same routine. "Get to the line, receive the ball, bounce it a few times, get your grip, bend your knees as you inhale deeply and let it out as you come up through your body in one straight motion and follow through on your shot". Coach Grant stressed believing that all your Free throws would go in. Focus on the rim. Disregard the hecklers, the other team, the fans, the score board, the time and everything else. Just follow your rhythm and steps. Many games are won or lost at the free throw line according to Coach Grant.

Coach Grant said in a perfect world (the movies) the guy hits all the free throws and the crowd goes wild. In the real world we try to hit as many as we can and keep moving forward. The key words are practice, practice, practice and give it your best.

Coach Grant gave each of the team members tips on their shooting and their form. He filled out an evaluation sheet on each player and gave them a copy.

Then it was break time for an hour. When they restarted practice there were scrimmages set up on the various courts. Coaches wanted to see how people played together and how they performed with total strangers. It was 5 on 5 pickup ball. Coaches looked at everything related to the players. Who meshed, who did not? Who could ball handle with ease and who could not handle the rock? The scrimmage on Julian's court came to a halt when he took flight from the foul line with one of his "The HAMMER" dunks. They looked at how high he had gotten and the force with which he rammed the ball through the hoop. Guys were high fiving him and commenting "good dunk". Some stood in awe just replaying it in their minds. When play resumed; two minutes in Julian went to the top of the square to catch an alley-oop pass and power it through the rim. Again, play was stopped as players howled and whooped it up about it. Julian's team was put on the sidelines and a new five were put in the game.

On the sidelines the teams were commenting on how high Julian would go. He would not comment. He left the conversation up to others.

There was another half hour break and then the players began mid-range and long-distance shooting drills. Later it was layup lines again and then stretching. As players and some coaches began to leave Brian and Julian began their usual drill of free throw shooting and jump shots along with skipping drills. They also had to add in more pushups and weight-lifting to add bulk up top.

A few coaches and players came over to speak with Julian. They said they had seen the video and thought the film was doctored. Now after having seen "The HAMMER" dunk in person they were glad that Julian was on their team. He shook hands with all of them and laughed. Julian and Brian finished their drills and headed to the cafeteria. They found a distant corner and settled in. After eating it was time to go to the library and begin to get in the habit of putting in study time. Brian and Julian wanted to be ahead as much as possible in their classes. They wanted to do what had worked for them to this point. What had worked for the two of them was giving extra effort in class and working out extra in practice. They would need every edge that they could get to stay ahead of their competitors at the "U".

After studying for an hour-plus they headed to their apartments. Julian dropped Brian off in front of his building and then cruised to his.

Julian received an email from his Mother and one from Miss Roslyn Ramirez the Lead Student Counselor. His mom was teasing Julian that now he would have to dial it up even more to keep up in College. Remember everyone in College was decent or good in High School. She reminded Julian that he was just as good or better than them so give it his all. He sent a reply that the message was received. He also told her that he had dropped "The Hammer" a couple of times in practice to let the other players know who they were dealing with. He sent an email response to Miss Ramirez that yes, he had gotten all the classes he wanted and was ok. Julian thanked her for her concern and care. He would never forget her for it.

Julian caught a shower and looked over his schoolwork and the written review of his shooting by the coach. He was not going to fall behind on his schoolwork. Julian studied his notes and the chapters they had read in the business class. He read a few chapters ahead to make sure that he was on target. He emailed Rachel and Pablo to make sure that things were going ok with the web site program. Rachel replied immediately. She wanted to make sure that Julian was taking his vitamins and pushing just as hard as in High School. She said her dream and prayer was to see him make it to the NBA as a first-round draft pick. Rachel and Pablo remained ardent supporters of Julian. They wanted him to do well at the "U".

The Williams family also sent an email asking Julian to look out for Brian and to keep him out of trouble. Julian sent an email back to them promising to do all he could for Brian. Later Julian set his alarm clock to get up and work on his 50 sit ups, 50 pushups and 50 crunches. He checked his locks and turned off the lights. He was tired. He went straight to sleep.

In New York Samantha White was rehashing what could have been with her and Julian. A cousin was reading the story of Julian's team winning the state championships. They story said he was now attending the University of Miami on a full scholarship. She began to get upset but then realized that it was all her fault and she would have to live with that. She was learning that her decision to "give Ron a taste" that one night was costing her millions.

They story went on to say how if Julian played anywhere near the way he played this past year in High School he was a certain first round NBA pick. As a first-round draft pick in the NBA he would be guaranteed millions. Samantha started to cry but she remembered the words that Rachel had told her when she had decided to mess around with Ron. Rachel had pleaded with her to either tell Julian or not to do it. Rachel told Samantha that she knew Julian had had a crush on her for a long, long, long time. Rachel had told her to tell Julian it was over if she was going to see someone else. When Rachel found out Samantha was sleeping with Ron; she told Samantha to never call her again. She told Samantha that she was blocking her and wanted nothing to do with her. Rachel told Samantha that someday she would regret what she had done. She told her to lose her number. Rachel blocked her phone number and blocked social media contact with Samantha White. Rachel would see Samantha in the hallway and go the other way at school. She was very relieved when Samantha left Marietta for New York.

"...Most Valuable Player..."

On the fifth day of practice at "the U" the basketball squad was cut down to 40 players. Many of those hoping to walk-on were told they were not making it. The next cut to 22 players would take place in two weeks. The participants had a chance to prove their worth in two-weeks before the final cuts would be made. Julian and Brian were not worried about making the team. They decided when they first got to campus that they would let their "play" do their talking for them.

Brian was doing his thing as a rebounder and put back scorer. Julian had worked and worked on his mid-range jumper and now it was paying off. When the defenders clogged the lanes he would dash down the lane and stop short and pull up. If they were not quick enough; he was to the hoop and dunking before they could call for help.

Brian and Julian were also getting to know their future teammates. They spoke to anyone that spoke with them. If the person did not speak; well that was how you were treated from that moment on. If you did not speak initially then both of them would leave you to your own devices. They also did not go out of their way to tell you what you did wrong and to shoot when you were reluctant to do so. Brian and Julian had the rule; speak once to you no response ok. Speak twice to you and no response; you were done. The two men were about business. They both wanted to make the team. They also wanted to be on a team that was going to go farther than the last one. The Hurricanes had lost in the first round of the NIT tournament. This year the team was playing a tougher schedule and if they came out with a solid win-loss record they were more than likely into the NCAA field. Time would tell.

Julian and Brian continued to work diligently on their mid-range scoring and rebounding. Each night they spent extra time practicing their mid-range jump shots as well as going to the Library to study.

Brian teased Julian about only being in school for one year but Julian would not respond.

In his heart and mind Julian wanted to complete his degree. He made a mental note to complete his degree online once he left school. Right now, his major was Business Management.

Two weeks later the last cuts to the team were made. Brian and Julian were not one of the ten casualties. Julian asked for and got the number 13 he wanted. Brian asked for number 8 and received it. After the cuts there was a huge team meeting and it was stressed to everyone that this is a "TEAM GAME". Coach Hall stressed that the team is the sum of all its parts. He stressed that like a chain with a weak link if we are not all equal parts strong; we will lose and go no- where. He stressed that it has to be "TEAM FIRST" and the accolades and personal stuff would come later.

Head Coach, Terry Hall stressed that the team was playing a tough 16 game schedule but that is how the Program and them would get better. His favorite saying became "to be the best you have to beat the BEST". The first game for the team would be an away game at Kentucky. It was going to be a war as Kentucky always got some of the top recruits to attend their school. Kentucky was well known for its NBA former players and top business alumni. The Hurricane team was getting "baptism under fire" with that first game. After that game it would still be good teams for the next four games. The Coaches, Alumni, team really wanted to beat instate rival Florida State University in that fifth game of the season at their house.

Coach Hall had played for Arkansas and was familiar with the phrase "40 minutes of hell". Arkansas was known for full court pressure the entire game. They would send a team of five out to start the game and then send in another team of five all game long. Coach Hall played in that system and he believed like Coach

Randle at Julian's High School a full-court-press caused teams to make mistakes. The Hurricanes would be a full court pressing team. Coach Hall stressed that it would take time for the team to get it right. The team began practicing the 2-2-1 full court press. They also worked against the 2-2-1 press and 1-2-2 press. It is said that teams which press do not like to be pressed. The Hurricanes figured by the fourth game against Boston College they would be ready. The Hurricanes would play their first home game against Northwestern.

The Hurricanes would have to go all out to win that game to get their fans motivated and behind them 100 percent. Northwestern would be bringing a new team to the game so they were both about even in that department. The advantage the Hurricanes had was that they would be playing at home. Coach Hall told the team to take each game as they came and not to look ahead.

Game one saw the Hurricanes get baptized by "fire". The Kentucky Wildcats were hot from the start. The Hurricanes fought back and got within five at half time. Julian was all over the place; blocking shots, rebounding, driving to the basket, bringing the ball up court and diving into the stands to save balls. He, Brian, Paul and the center Max ended up with floor burns and bruises from hitting seats in the bleachers.

Julian leapt over the first row of seats into the aisle behind them to save a Miami Hurricane possession. The young Hurricanes came up 12 points short losing 101-89 to Kentucky. The team had not seen half court pressure like the pressure Kentucky applied to them. The double team was coming from the guards, center and sometimes the wing. As Coach Hall stated it was a learning experience. The team relaxed after the game in their hotel and left the next day for Wake Forest. This time the team came out on the winning end of the game. The Hurricanes got their first taste of victory with a 9-point win over Wake Forest. They returned home to get ready for their first home game against Northwestern. Having had a taste of victory against Wake Forest the team was hyped to play their next game.

Every practice the Hurricane Coaching staff placed an emphasis on the 2-2-1 press. They had to get turnovers. They had to get rebounds. They had to get to the rim on their drives. They could not afford silly turnovers and sloppy ball movement. They could not afford lazy fouls. They could not give up easy shots. They had to contest every shot. The Mid-range area will be open for shots if we move the ball quickly. Keep cutting across and from the low post up and out foul line extended. The coach had all of the team members work on their mid-range shots and foul shots.

Coach Hall told the team from the film in the last part of their game the Northwestern team would resort to reaching and fouling. They did not move their feet well in the end of the third and fourth quarters. He also spoke with the guards and let them know that they needed to feed Paul, Max, Brian and Julian.

The coach believed that if the Hurricanes could get out on the run against the Northwestern team they had the advantage. We have fast floor runners that can also handle the ball and will make shots. We also have Paul, Max and Julian that will go high to get your lob passes and convert them. Coach Hall stressed to the team that to win against Northwestern they were going to have to be aggressive and start fast. He said the whole team has got to be active on defense and offense. If we are hesitant the Northwestern guards can score in bunches and will bury us in 3's. Coach Hall stated that the Northwestern team believes it is the Golden State Warriors of the NBA. They will start firing the minute they get over half court if they hit a few.

Coach Hall showed the team film of the Northwestern team in the third and fourth quarters of games. They were reaching and grabbing at players from the opposing team. He also showed film of the Northwestern team when they begin hitting their outside shots. They looked just like the Golden State Warriors. Coach Hall stated the answer to their problems was to put the pressure on them so that they cannot execute. If we apply the pressure right and get Paul, Max and Julian to hammer them a couple of times we will take their heart. Coach Hall said he does not have a problem with smart fouls. He has a problem with people not being in the right positions to press the other team. He showed them the hot shooting Northwestern team to remind them of what could happen if they do not do their jobs correctly as a team.

The team ran layup lines to end practice and then huddled. Coach Hall told them to be at the gym early to get taped and stretched. As the team left the coached asked Paul and Julian for a minute to speak with them. He told the two of them that they were going to have to carry the heavy load for the team. Paul will bring the ball up on offense along with you. The other guards will be on the wing to spot up and shoot. He gave the green light to Paul and Julian to do their thing. He stated that you both can handle the ball very well. He also stated that both of you have the ability to go high above the rim. Coach told them to work together and "Make things HAPPEN" for the team. The three shook hands and left.

Julian rushed to get his stuff together. He wanted to catch a short nap before the game. The game was at 8:30pm and the coaching staff wanted them there forty minutes early. It was already 4pm. Julian had had one class today. Brian had none. Julian collected Brian and they headed for the Silver Bullet. They tossed their stuff in the back of the car and headed out. They were a bit nervous about their first home-game but they did not talk about it. Brian reminded Julian that due to it being a home game they were going to have to get there earlier. Julian figured he would sleep for an hour and about 7pm head for the gym. The two agreed to call the other and make sure they got up. Julian set both his clocks and crawled into bed. He had already gotten his sweat suit, game sneakers, socks, underwear, tights and stuff ready. When the clock alarms went off Julian called Brian and told him he was up and getting a shower. He showered and made himself some pancakes. He dressed quickly and ate.

Julian grabbed his gym bag and made sure that he had everything that he needed. Julian made sure that he had his phone, car keys and wallet. He called Brian to tell him that he was on the way. Brian told him he was out front waiting. Also waiting is Paul Wood. He lives on the same floor with me. I told him we could all ride together. See you shortly said Julian.

Julian put his bag in the trunk and raced over to Brian's building. He popped the trunk to let Brian and Paul put their gym bags into the trunk. It was a ten to fifteen-minute ride to the gym most nights but tonight it took half an hour. They told security who they were. Julian followed a security officer on a golf cart to an area designated for the players and coaches to park. The players hustled to the gym. First stop, getting taped up to protect the ankles. Next stop the bathroom. Stretch a bit and then dress in team shorts and sweatpants. Keep on hoodie and warm up. Shoot around time and then layup lines. The gym is packed to full capacity. There are alumni and local celebrities on hand including the Mayor of Miami.

The team then is called back into the dressing room to get ready for the game. Julian looks at Brian and say's "this is it"! In the dressing room the team members put on their jerseys and wrist bands. They get ready for the start of the game. Coach Hall tells the team to get ready; they are going to press and press and press some more. They line up. The starters are told. The announcer already has the list. The teams come out to wild cheers from the capacity crowd.

They run their lay-up lines. The Last man on the line is Julian and he soars for his Michael Jordan dunk. People start jumping up and down. Then it's introduction time. After the hyped-up player introductions; it's game time.

The Hurricanes win the jump ball as Maxwell Strong taps the ball to Julian. He crosses over his man and lobs to a soaring Paul Wood.

Full court press results in Northwestern trying a long pass that is stolen by Brian. He gets it to Maxwell in the middle and he lobs to Julian. Julian brings the ball straight through the rim to the floor for another two points. Three quick turnovers result in two three pointers and one layup. Northwestern calls a time out. Coach Hall tells Julian, Paul, Max, Brian and the rest of the team to get ready. The game is about to become very physical from this point. Don't argue or get caught up retaliating. Let the refs call the game. Let me handle the refs and bad players he tells the team. Sure enough elbows begin flying. Grabbing and pulling begins. Coach Hall has already talked to the officials and they are paying attention. Two more turnovers and scores by Miami. Northwestern has only had two points scored. The score is 21 to 9 with ten minutes gone in the first half. Northwestern calls another time out. Out of the time out Northwestern finally is able to break the press and score on a long three. They score one more time on a long three and Coach Hall uses a time out to make two substitutions. He puts in fresh guards for the point of the press. He puts Paul back in the game and takes out another sophomore player. He moves Julian to one forward and Brian on the other side of Max. He tells the team that they have to keep Northwestern from getting hot.

Julian single handedly takes matters into his own hands. He moves Max to one of the wing spots and he mans the middle. A Northwestern player starts to drive on Brian. Julian blocks his shot into the second row. A Northwestern forward pulls up and Julian starts a fast break with his block. Max collects it. Passes to Paul and back to Brian for a lay-up. Another turnover and Paul tosses a lob to the top of the square Julian brings it straight through the rim and to the floor "BLAMMMMMM". There is pandemonium. The gym goes wild.

The Coach of Northwestern calls his final time out. The crowd is now on its feet and the gym is rocking. Coach Hall tells the team we are going to press all night. He pulls Julian, Max and Paul. He sends in three veterans (Juniors and Seniors). They begin to press and make three more quick turnovers and scores. Finally, it is half time. At Half time Coach Hall says the first half starters will start again. We have to keep pressing. He designates a whole different five to be ready to go

in and another five to go in after that. Coach Hall says if we keep the lead large everyone plays. If the lead goes down then we will return Paul, Julian, Brian and the other starters. He stressed it was up to the players who play to make it easier for him to send in the others. When play resumed it was more of the same. The "U" kept the pressure on. Turnover after turnover and it was a blowout. Julian and Brian had a successful coming out party. The gym was rocking right up to the end. The final score was 109 – 71. Players were dancing, cheerleaders were dancing, spectators were dancing and even the coach was in the middle of the circle getting "his dance on" and doing his thing at the end of the game.

Coach held a quick meeting of the team and told them that they had done an amazing job the last two games. They needed to keep moving forward. Next game would be at the home of Boston College in two weeks. Then it is off to FSU ten days after that game for a game there. You know that the Boston College team already knows that we won. They will be more than eager to beat us. Relax tonight and tomorrow. Enjoy the win. We practice again in three days. The team and their fans gave a big cheer. The DJ cranked up the music and everyone had a good time.

There was lots of food, Gatorade, water, fruit and snacks. The Northwestern team and their coaches remained for a while after the game and they spoke with the coaches and players of the Hurricanes. The coaches spoke with Julian and could not believe what they had read and heard. They asked Julian to tell them (himself) that he was the bench jockey the year before last at his high school. His girl leaves him; and he becomes "the Dark Knight". He leads his team to the state championship title last year after not even playing in most games the year before. Everyone asks Julian how did that happen? He tells them truly that in practice the year before he was playing above average but when the game buzzer sounded, he played badly. So, he rode the pine. Only if it was a blow-out loss or win did he get to play. Julian told them last year and how I play now is because my brother says after my girl left me; I dedicated myself to getting better in all phases of my b-ball game. Julian said when his girl left him for another guy instead of getting mad at them; I would get mad at the rims I have bent and hammered with my dunks. Some of the Northwestern team reserves could not believe Julian's story and what they read and saw on the internet. Julian said it is 100% true.

Julian told them all that the stories on the internet and in the magazines are 100% true. Before last year; in the games I could hardly catch the ball. I could dunk before but not like I can now. I jumped rope every day and still do. I bought those crazy shoes that they have on TV to improve your vertical. They really work. I practiced and practiced and practiced some more. I also studied the best in the NBA league now and in the past.

Julian said he studied Magic, Bird, MJ, Dominique, The Iceman, KG, Dennis Rodman, Shawn Kemp, Stefan Curry, Klay Thompson, Lebron, Kyrie Irving, Dr. J and many others. He said he also studied the And1 players and their tour mixtapes. He said he pulled a little bit from this one and a little from that one. He said his "THE HAMMER" dunk is the perfect example. He said the dunk is parts of three different dunks. It is MJ and Dr. J taking off from the free throw line. It is Dominique and Vince Carter at full throttle and it is Shawn Kemp's behind the head throw down all rolled into one. The group said wow that is where that dunk comes from. They all laughed. One of the Northwestern players said when he first saw it he said "Whoa; what kind of dunk is that?"

Julian pointed at Brian and said he was the one that gave it "The HAMMER" name. I did it for him when we met at camp. Someone filmed it and placed it on the internet. We did not know until the All-Star game. Michael Jordan even called me. I have his number in my phone. Really??? Julian pulled out his phone and showed them MJ's name. He called me after I won the MVP at the All-Star game at the Rachel camp. He called me again after the State High School Championship game MVP award.

Julian said the bottom line is if you dedicate yourself you can do anything. He said he remembered the story that coaches say all the time. They say when you are out partying, goofing off, not practicing hard there is a guy out there putting in the work. He is training and practicing when you are sleep. He is training and practicing when you are partying or being lazy and when you meet him; he will destroy you. Julian said he bets after the All-Star game a lot of the players he played against began to practice and train harder. He said he remembered in the first half when he took off on one guy; he could see the shock in his face when I put the ball behind my head to slam it. He bailed out quickly.

Julian said he never keeps track of how many dunks he makes or who he dunks on. But know this when I head to the rim, I am remembering my girl leaving me and the guy she left me for. Every rim is them. That is my motivation and will always be my motivation. Julian answered their questions on training, nutrition and the need to stretch constantly. Several of the northwestern team members and reserves exchanged numbers with Julian and his teammates.

Soon it was time to head home. Julian rounded up Brian and Paul. They headed home. Julian dropped Paul and Brian off to their building. He headed to his building and raced to his apartment. He pulled off his clothes and filled his tub with hot water and Epsom Salt. He had to soak for a while. He was now feeling the soreness from the game. He soaked until the water became cold.

Julian let the water run out of the tub then he took a hot/cold shower. He started out hot and then made the water hotter until he could not stand it. Then he turned the water cold and colder until he could not stand it. He took a warm shower and then he dressed for bed. Julian crawled beneath the sheets with a smile on his face. He had won in front of his fans and now the team was gaining a following. Julian was out like a light as fatigue caught up with him. He had no classes the next day until the late afternoon. Julian figured he would spend most of the day in bed. He owed it to himself to take care of himself. Resting his body was crucial.

In Marietta Mrs. Baxter was busy taking calls from friends and family members as they showed highlights of Julian and the Hurricanes stomping Northwestern's basketball team. They showed Julian and the mean look on his face as he took off to dunk on two Northwestern players that were foolish enough to jump with him. Randall was all smiles as he turned in after hearing the reports of Julian's Hurricanes winning big over Northwestern. Next up for them was Boston College. This was going to be a tougher test for Julian and his team.

Julian was proving to the college world that he "was the real deal".

"...Most Valuable Player..."

Coach Terry Hall said a prayer of thanks as he climbed into bed. He loved his team's total effort. They hustled, they rebounded well. They applied full court pressure just like he and his teammates did during their college days at Arkansas. Julian was proving to be a god-send. He was firing up the troops and leading by example. He blocked the shot of the 7-footer for Northwestern.

The next day the campus of the "U" was on fire about the team's beatdown of Northwestern. Fans were talking about the team's hustling and effort in the win. Previous teams were lethargic. This team was explosive. Several of the players had had thunderous dunks in the game; Joseph, Max, Paul, Tyrone, Brian, Victor and Julian. The students did not care if the team lost as long as they gave the same effort all the time.

The national media was saying wait until they play Boston College to see how they held up. Two weeks later on the flight to Boston the coaches stressed to the team that this is their version of world war III. The media and everyone else are all saying that you will lose and lose badly. The coaches said we are going to do the same thing that we did against Northwestern. We are going to press, press and press some more. Paul said each player would have to push it to their limits because that was the only way they were going to win. The coaches reminded the guards on defense that the Boston College guards can really shoot. If they get hot, we will go to a man to man defense for a time to throw them off and then switch back to full court 2-2-1 pressure. Coach told the team if you get tired raise your hand and we will put someone else in for you for a time. If we pull you then you stay on the bench with us.

The coach set up three teams of five and kept switching them out. It was over in the first half. The Hurricanes racked up turnover after turnover and converted them to fast-break points.

At half time the score was 51 – 30 in favor of the Hurricanes. Julian and Paul were everywhere causing turnovers or picking off passes. When Boston College attempted their "much vaunted" long distance shooting they were closely contested. The Hurricanes had switched to man-to-man right after Boston College hit their first two in row long distance shots. The Hurricanes led by Brian, Joseph, Julian and Max were cleaning up any shots that made it to the boards for Boston College. The Hurricane starters got the rest of the night off in the middle of the second half. They cheered and acted as coaches for their other teammates.

It was a good old-fashioned blow-out. The final score of 112-67 was no indicator of how bad the Boston College team was in handling the full court pressure. Coach Hall urged his starters to take advantage of the rest to start applying ice as the last quarter was being played. Paul, Julian, Max, Joseph, Brian and Victor had ice applied to their knees and ankles at the end of the bench. The coach wanted them to get a head start on healing because they were going to be in a real physical game at FSU. Instead of two weeks they were only going to have ten days. They needed to be ready quickly.

After the game the team quickly boarded the buses and headed to the airport. Instead of staying overnight there in Boston the charter would leave for Florida and the Florida State game right away. They would arrive early; heal, practice and get ready for the game there. They would have two days to rest and heal then practice would resume at a nearby Junior college.

The team rested as they flew through the skies to Florida from the northeast corridor. The coaches made sure that the team members were all wrapped up in blankets to retain their body heat. Coaches were running about making sure the players drank lots of Gatorade and water. Fresh ice packs were applied to all team members that needed them. A couple players with strains were given electronic stimulation and massages. For the most part the team ate, slept and drank their fluids.

At the hotel the team members were paired off. Brian and Julian usually roomed together on the road. They both went straight to bed after getting to their room. The coaches had pass keys to get in all the rooms. They checked on all the players after two hours to see if someone needed extra help. Everyone was pretty much ok. Team doctors made sure that no one had any serious injuries. Coach Hall told the team to rest an extra day. The practices would start on Thursday with walk through's and press coverage. They would work on changing the press attack to a 3-1-1 or 1-2-2 from time to time against FSU as well as going to man-to-man. Coach put together a short video on man-to-man coverage by Villanova in the NCAA championship game. They were able to avoid switching with good communication and hustle. The coaches showed the game and how Villanova overplayed their men and caused havoc on their way to the championship game win.

Julian would be in the middle of the 3-1-1 press. He would play behind Joseph, Paul and Brian. Max would be the last man. In the 2-2-1 Julian would play on the second line of the 2's and it would be up to him and Victor to back up Brian and Paul. In the man to man coverage Julian always took the other team's best player.

The team knew that FSU was going to be tough to beat. The in-state rivalry was important to the "U" alumni. This was a "MUST WIN". Julian told the guards that during the game as long as it was in the vicinity of the rim or backboards he, Paul, Max and Brian would go get it.

Watch our eyes, head movement and arm movements. If I point to the rim send it and don't worry about who is on me said Julian. We have to get this win and we will if we think with no limits. Back cuts and baseline movement will be key especially in the third and fourth quarters of the game Coach Hall told his players. The team worked on a variation of the 1-4 wide that Julian's team used in high school. The difference is Julian would be on the baseline. He had the freedom to cut to the middle or stay on the baseline.

To give FSU something to think about Coach Hall had the Hurricanes pickup at half court and play man-to-man. FSU ran a lot of screens and held a 5-point lead midway through the first half. FSU got a lob dunk over Paul and then another one over Julian.

Coach Hall called a time out as the FSU players began pointing at Julian and Paul. The FSU fans began to chant the mystery dunker got dunked on by FSU. Julian said nothing but Brian knew he was getting dialed in. In the huddle Julian asked coach to let them go back to full court pressure and the 2-2-1 press. Julian told the guards just throw it to the square above the basket; Paul, Max and I will show them what time it is.

After the time out there was a technical foul called on one of the FSU players for teasing Paul and Julian. At the seven-minute mark the Hurricanes' full court press began to have an effect. One turnover and Brian got an easy dunk. A Second turnover and Paul took flight and gave the crowd something to think about. A short time later the FSU crowd was silenced. Paul got a steal and flipped it to Julian on the run. Julian took off just past the free throw line and jackhammered a two-handed dunk to the floor over their best player. You could hear the crowd take a deep breath as they played it again on the jumbo screen. You could clearly see the power and the rage in the slam. Julian said nothing to the FSU player he just turned and ran to his position in the press. On the next turnover Julian lobbed the ball to Max and he brought the curtain down on the FSU team. Game over. After half time Coach Terry Hall decided to hit FSU with full court pressure in waves of five. It was all over;

the second and third teams played most of the last quarter of the game. FSU fans were leaving as they could not close the gap. The lead stayed at 19 points until the buzzer sounded; game over.

The fans of the University of Miami stormed the FSU court and started jumping around, dancing and having a good time. There were a ton of Police Officers and Security to ensure that the fans had a good time and there were no skirmishes. After jumping around with the fans for a little while; members of the Hurricanes basketball team headed to the dressing room to relax. The Hurricane team members enjoyed the moment. The coaches kept telling the players to enjoy and savor the moment. Many other Hurricane teams had played FSU and lost over and over and over again.

Randall called Julian and congratulated him on the win once he found out. His mother, Rachel, Pablo and his father had already emailed or called him. Mrs. Baxter cautioned Julian to stay humble. She said the team was on a winning streak. She reminded Julian that wins and losses come in bunches. The key would be to take the losses and learn from them but not dwell on them too long. She reminded Julian that few teams go undefeated through the entire season. She said most teams get one, two, three or four losses in a season.

She also cautioned Julian that the regular season and the playoffs are totally different animals. The playoffs and championship series are cut-throat as one call can send a team sideways and out of the NCAA tournament or the NIT tournament. She reminded Julian that he was now only a third of the way into his team's schedule. She reminded him to get as much rest as possible. She and Randall reminded Julian to continually stretch before and after games as well as when he returned home. Mrs. Baxter also advised Julian to ice down all the time to avoid strains or tear injuries.

As a good son; Julian listened and took all the advice in from his mother. When he told Brian and Paul what his mother said they both gave him a hard time. Julian's defense was his mother was a basketball star in High School, College and the WNBA. Just like he observed and watched the NBA greats and others he also watched tape and DVD's of WNBA greats and legends. The team stayed over in Florida for an extra day of rest and relaxation. Julian took the time to go swimming with several other players in the ocean not too far away. They stretched and walked the beach. No running and no working out.

Rachel and Pablo celebrated as the viewership for the Julian Baxter Non-Profit web site went through the roof every time after the Hurricanes played. They were raising lots of funds. They donated to the Red Cross, Abused Women's Organizations, After School Programs and the Boys and Girls Clubs. Pablo and Rachel sent Julian an email congratulating him on his wins and the performance of the team to this point. They had also created new T-shirts with Julian on the Hurricanes team in uniform and they were selling like hotcakes.

Julian was remembering what Brian had talked about "building a legacy" by getting the University of Miami basketball program off the ground. He and the team members hoped by the wins and effort that they were giving people were looking at the team differently.

Even in their losses the Hurricanes were giving max effort in all areas. They had a couple of tough losses to Clemson and Syracuse in the middle of their season. Then the team brushed aside the University of Central Florida and Auburn basketball teams.

To end the regular season the Hurricanes went "toe to toe" with Duke and lost out by eight points. The team ended the season with a 12-4 record and on track to play in the NCAA tournament. The team was given two days to rest before practices resumed. Then came selection Sunday. The Hurricanes made the field. Paul, Brian, Max and Julian gave it their best effort and the team made it to the round of 16. In the sweet 16 the Hurricanes fought and scrapped to the end but lost to Michigan by three points on a desperation heave just before the end of the game.

For the year Julian had averaged 29 points, 12 rebounds, 8 assists and 5 blocks per game. He was named Most Valuable Player in the ACC region. Julian never gave the NBA any more thought after being told that he could possibly get there after High School. He figured things would take care of themselves if he worked hard, practiced hard and kept improving his game. It worked out well for him. Several scouting

Publications for the NBA were giving Julian the nod to go number one or in the top three of the upcoming draft. The Atlanta Hawks had the first pick in the draft and the New York Knicks were picking second with the Charlotte Hornets picking third.

All three teams could use a wing player like Julian with his ball handling and shooting skills. He also brought excellent defensive and rebounding skills to the table. Coach Hall was being told that the Atlanta Hawks were doing all that they could to lock down Julian as the number one pick. Julian's agent, Austin LaSalle of CAA Sports figured he was going number one by the interest after his workout with the Hawks.

The GM, the Head Coach, Assistant Coaches, Player Development Staff and owners were on hand for Julian's workout in Atlanta. There were more media (Internet, Radio, TV, Newspaper, Magazine, Blog, ESPN, TMZ and others) on hand for Julian's workout than at some of the games for the Hawks.

Julian chatted with the coaches and staff. He warmed up, stretched and then received his final instructions. Then after a few warmup shots it was time to audition for becoming the top pick in the draft. They had Julian make layups (left and right-handed). They had him shoot 10 free throws and then 10 jump shots from varying ranges. They measured his vertical jump - 52" inches. They took his weight, height and wingspan measurements. They wanted to see him rebound a bit. They had coaches throwing the ball to the backboards. Then they asked Julian to dunk a few shots to see his body motion and balance. One of the coaches asked at the end if Julian would do his foul-line "Hammer Dunk". Julian went past half court and looked at the Rim in the distance. The "incident" replayed itself in his mind and he started running towards the foul line. He took off from there and flew to the rim and hammered the ball through the rim straight to the floor "BLAMMMMMMMMM". With that slam he became the favorite to become the first choice in the draft.

Julian, his mother, his father, Randall, Brian, Rachel, Pablo, Coach Hall from the University of Miami and several neighbors were all invited to New York to be a part of Julian's group. At the draft night event in the Barclays Center in Brooklyn the group laughed and joked until the event started.

There was nervous energy throughout the room as they waited for the proceedings to get underway. Soon it was time for the picking of players. Then came the announcement they had all came to hear; with the first pick of the 2019 NBA Draft the Atlanta Hawks select from the University of Miami; Small Forward, Julian "The Mystery Dunker" Baxter. For a minute Julian just sat there in shock and then he got up and hugged his family, friends, neighbors and coach. His Agent, Austin LaSalle of Global Sports Agency appeared out of nowhere to give him a hug as he headed for the stage. On the stage Julian shook hands and got a hug from NBA Commissioner,

Adam Silver. A rep from the NBA handed Julian an Atlanta Hawks hat. Julian put it on and was then given an Atlanta Hawks jersey with the number 1 on it.

The media all snapped photos left and right. Then it was that stroll across the stage to the back where the remainder of the media waited to interview Julian. What once was a faint "possibility" had now become a "reality". Julian was asked how he felt. His response; gratified that the Hawks thought enough of him to make him the first choice and he would do all that he could to make the city, people of Marietta and his teammates proud.

Julian was asked if he had anything to say to Samantha White now that he was going to be a multimillionaire due to his NIKE shoe contract, his Mercedes Benz contract, his Rolex Watch contract, his Delta Airlines Contract, Men's Wearhouse, HP Computers, AT&T Cell Phones and Atlanta Hawks player contracts. Julian took the high road and said he wished her all the success that this life can offer.

Julian said yes, he did Love Samantha White at one time. That love died when he saw her behind the basketball gym at High School with another guy. He was moving forward with his life. He is not mad at her at all. She made her choice and I made mine to move forward and try to be the best human being, brother, son, neighbor, citizen, friend and basketball player that I can be. Yes, basketball will now bring me a lot of money. I plan to use the money to try to make a difference for young people, abused women, the homeless and to give college scholarships to the needy.

In Rochester, New York Samantha White was out with co-workers at a Sports Bar when her name and picture was shown on TV as the commentators were talking. One of her friends saw the photo and her name. They asked why her name and photo was up there.

She had to explain that in high school she had dated Julian for two years. He was a reserve player on the men's basketball team. She was constantly being pursued by Ron who was the starting quarterback for the football team. At the end of year dance and concert she had foolishly decided to give a "taste" to Ron. Julian had seen the whole thing but never revealed himself. He had shut down all contact with me and changed his whole persona. He was a good basketball player in practice but after that he began to show-out and destroy people on the basketball court. He became a Superstar and tonight he got drafted number one and now they are bringing me up again. Hopefully for the last time. Samantha White admitted to her friends that she had really messed up; but it was already done. She had to do the best that she could.

Foolishly she had messed up on Julian who adored her for a fling with a football star and left a Superstar in the making. So now, Julian was having the last laugh. I tried to apologize to him; but he has not said one word beyond "Hi, Bye and Busy". One of the girls said you can't blame him. He saw you and the other guy. He did not hear about it from someone; he actually witnessed you making out with someone.

You and the guy are lucky he did not go crazy and kill both of you. If I was a man in that situation, I would not speak with you anymore myself. Samantha said, "she gets it now" and will have to live with the regret. She said this is a night she could have been beside Julian and enjoying the moment. Life goes on she said and walked away from her friends towards the bathroom. Samantha did not want her friends to see the tears streaming down her face. One bad choice and now her life trajectory has been changed forever. She could not dwell on what could have been she now had to keep moving forward. Ron had been hurt in two of the football games. He had also been the subject of multiple attacks by people that liked Julian. He had moved to the Midwest area to get his life together. He kept in touch from time to time. If she had only listened to Rachel. Rumor was that Rachel and Pablo were now working with Julian on his web site and charity Foundation. They saw the future success of Julian while she was blinded by beauty, sex, vanity, ego and popularity.

At the party in New York after being named number one the Atlanta Hawks called to let Julian know a private jet would be picking him up in the morning and bringing him and his agent to Atlanta. They wanted to wrap this matter up and have a press conference right away. Julian said no problem he would be ready. The Hawks called his agent and gave him the necessary instructions and information.

A short time later his agent Austin LaSalle appeared and asked for a quiet moment with Julian and his parents. He confirmed that they would both be flying out to Atlanta tomorrow morning. Two other members of the Global Sports Agency team would also be going with us. We will be staying downtown at the W Hotel. They want to hammer out an agreement as soon as possible and then find a center to complement the team. My team's job is to get you the best possible deals on all things. We work to protect your interest. We have already secured the various agreements with Mercedes, Rolex, Delta Airlines, Men's Wearhouse, HP Computers, AT&T Cellphones, NIKE, SunTrust Bank, Go Daddy and QT Service Stations. Coca-Cola is after us to become their spokesman for their water division knowing your big thing on drinking lots of water. Kroger, Publix, State Farm, Progressive, Wellstar, LA Fitness, Allstate and Windy Hill Fitness Centers have all submitted bids to have Julian as their spokesperson. Austin LaSalle told Julian and his family that the plan is to hold off on any more sponsorships until after the Hawks sign you up. Remember there is a scale that was set up in the NBA players Collective Bargain Agreement.

Austin LaSalle told Julian to expect $41,242,888 in a four-year deal and we would have to negotiate a fifth year. There would be an

$18,000,000 guarantee in the contract. The fifth year could be as much as a 20 to 25% increase over the previous four year's salary. We will work with you and the team to get the best deal possible. We expect that fifth-year salary to be in the $12.5 to $16.5 million-dollar range. That is what we will be shooting for. All other sponsorships will be looked at strategically after the contract with Atlanta is signed. Julian and his family agreed with the strategy proposed by Austin LaSalle and his Global Sports Agency team.

Austin LaSalle and Global Sports Agency had already more than proven his worth with all the top-notch agreements for sponsorship with Julian. He had also gotten the sponsors to donate to the non-profit Foundation as well for the next three years. Julian was winning all around. Now to phase three of his life plan; play in the NBA and along the way he would find a life partner.

For some reason Rachel detected a distant look in Julian's gaze after the meeting with Austin LaSalle and his parents. She felt something was not right based on her history with Julian. She asked him to take a walk with her; she had a few "private questions" for him. Rachel and Pablo were the ones that knew him when he was a midget and not a number one draft choice and now multi-millionaire. That was why Julian completely trusted Rachel and Pablo.

They went to the elevator and took it to the rooftop pool area and looked out over the New York/New Jersey expanse and the skyline. Rachel was quiet around strangers but with her friends she was extremely direct. She let them know exactly how she felt. She asked Julian what was bothering him? Is it Samantha White; she asked him? He said in the back of his mind the night would have been complete if we were still together. Julian told Rachel he always wondered if there was something that he could have done to have kept her from cheating? Rachel said there was "absolutely nothing that he could have done to change things". Rachel took Julian by the hand and pulled him to a large pool chair. They sat side by side as Rachel told Julian to look her in the eye and tell her if he ever thought about cheating on Samantha White? Julian said no; never crossed his mind. Julian told Rachel that it caught him by total surprise to see Samantha having sex with Ron behind the gymnasium.

Julian told Rachel his first impulse was to grab a piece of wood that was nearby and beat them both into dust but decided against it. He said he just let the tears fall and waited until they left to walk home. He did not want to see anyone.

Rachel told Julian that he had done everything right as far as she could see. She told Julian to stop looking back and look forward. Look around at all the positive ways you are giving hope, inspiration and encouragement to so many. Take a deep breath and savor the good things you are doing and your amazing achievements. From the end of the bench to starter to state champ to College and putting the University of Miami on the map for basketball to now being the number one draft pick in the NBA. Rachel told Julian to stop looking back and enjoy life. Stop thinking of what if and deal with the NOW. You are only promised today. Look at the happy faces of your family, neighbors, coaches, former teammates and also know that you are getting your revenge on Samantha and Ron now. They are probably miserable as all get out right now. Especially Samantha White is feeling the heat. Just like some men cannot pass up someone or say no and stay faithful to one-woman Samantha White is like that.

Rachel told Julian a story that she had heard. She said in a car, truck or other vehicle the front windshield is way, way, way bigger than the rearview mirror because they only want you to "glance" in the rear and keep your main focus on the road ahead. Rachel told Julian having grown up with him she knew how he was. She wanted him to keep working hard on his basketball skills; but she also wanted him to take time out to travel and enjoy some of the money. Rachel urged Julian to go and do some things for his old schools, former teammates, neighborhood kids and have a huge block party in the neighborhood.

Rachel told Julian he can change things for a lot of people so go make it happen. Invest in small businesses. Some of your friends and teammates did not make it to the NBA; give them a helping hand. Go spend some of that money and remember your "poorer friends..." hint, hint, hint. Julian started laughing at Rachel. She was also cracking up. She said I guess as you promised; once the money hits the bank Pablo and I get to be paid for our work full time. "Did I say that...?" said Julian. Rachel said oh yes you promised you would do that; and your Mom is a witness. Julian said you had to bring my Mom into this. Why not said Rachel. She also wants to get paid for her time and work. Does that mean I have to give you guys a bonus or back pay for all the time you have put in up to now Julian asked Rachel? She said we all hoped that you would be considerate of the time and energy that we put into getting the web site and Foundation started. Julian said he was indeed considerate and would be giving each of them $50,000.00 as a bonus for their work up to now. He would be giving a $25,000.00 bonus to the three salaried workers that were also there. He would be setting up a proper office. He would also pay for revamping the web site and putting $300,000.00 in the Foundation account to get it moving forward.

Thank you for always keeping me on the right track Julian told Rachel. He put his arm around her and gave her a big hug. Even when I was acting a fool you kept checking on me along with Pablo. Rachel said that is what being a friend is about. Being a friend does not mean we will always agree on things Rachel told Julian. Julian asked Rachel why he had never seen her out with someone?

Rachel said he did not see her because he was too wild-eyed about Samantha White. She was the only person he could see at that time.

Rachel told Julian she is a private person. She said she had dated a couple of older guys; but those relationships went nowhere. She was waiting for Mr. Right to show up and sweep her off her feet. She said she would know that he is the one by how he treats me; and I would never cheat on him. Rachel said her man would send her flowers and cards every day and let her know that he valued her highly. Julian told Rachel not to forget to send him an invitation when she hooked up with "Mr. Right. Rachel said on a second thought no; she would not invite him, Pablo or Randall. She told Julian that she knew Randall had had a crush on her before and then it faded out. Rachel said to the three of them she had moved into the "friend area" so no one was interested in dating her. Many people openly said I was gay in High School. I just ignored them all. Rachel told Julian in time the right man will come along and find out what a precious jewel I am. But we are here to talk about "YOU" Julian not me; Rachel told him.

Rachel told Julian from the bottom of her heart she was very, very, very happy for him and his success. Now she wants to see him happy too. She told Julian you have my number to call me anytime you want to talk. I will expect my bonus by the end of next week so that I can get a new car. She got up and started doing a little shimmy shake dance and ended it with a spin and high kick.

Julian started laughing his head off. I never knew you danced. Well, Mr. Baxter when you were busy practicing and playing basketball; I was taking jazz, tap and ballet lessons. Gotcha!!! She told Julian. At that remark Julian got up and took Rachel's hand and gave her a twirl and told her "I Apologize" for not keeping track of you. Rachel looked Julian directly in the eyes and said, "Apology accepted".

Rachel took Julian's hand and tugged at him to come with her and get back to his party before they send a search party out looking for him. As they rode down to the ballroom area Julian told Rachel "thanks again for knowing me and always being there". "You are always welcome Rachel told him". Mrs. Baxter rushed up to Julian when he walked in and gave him a big hug. The Global Sports Agency Photographer told Rachel and Mrs. Baxter to put Julian between them and took photos of them. He then had the whole group come together for a series of photos. Julian asked for a photo of him and Rachel together alone. Then a photo of him and Pablo alone, him and Brian alone and him and Randall alone and then one of the family together. Julian asked for a photo with him and his agent Austin LaSalle alone. Then the whole group gathered for a series of photos. Julian asked for the photographer's business card as he might want some special prints made.

A huge multi-layer cake was brought in on a tray by the hotel staff and it said "Congratulations to the Number One pick in the NBA draft – Julian "The Mystery Dunker" Baxter. Julian was called up to cut the cake. He teased that it almost seems like a wedding tonight. He cut a huge piece of cake then cut it up again into three pieces. One piece for Mom, One piece for Dad and another piece for Randall. The second piece that he cut was also extra-large. He cut the second piece of cake into three pieces and called up Rachel, Brian and Pablo to give it to them. Then he cut a third large piece of cake and cut that in three pieces and gave one piece to Coach Hall, one to his agent Austin LaSalle and the other piece he had it boxed. He was sending that third piece to Coach Randle. He invited all the remaining guests to come up. He gathered a stack of plates and cut a piece for each one of them. Julian thanked each and every guest.

Julian asked for a round of applause for his Mom, Pablo and Rachel for their work on his Non-Profit Foundation. Julian also announced "so that Rachel will not be mad at me and give me the weird eye look" effective immediately Pablo, Rachel and my Mom will be paid for their work with the Non-Profit Foundation in my name. The entire team would be receiving one-time bonuses for the work that they have done with the Foundation to this point. "Thank you to each member of the Non-Profit team and especially, Mom, Pablo and Rachel for your great work. We can and we will do more" Julian told the group. Rachel began laughing at Julian for his announcement. She gave him two thumbs up. His mother was doing the same to Julian. Julian said he would be taking a closer look at the facilities and the web site. The Non-Profit web site and facilities will all be updated. He was open to suggestions to do more in the community in all areas. Everyone gave Julian a rousing round of applause.

Mr. Baxter told his wife that he wished that instead of going after the "center of attention" females like Samantha White; Randall and Julian would go after the more well-rounded women like Rachel. Women like Rachel can see more than just themselves. Mr. Baxter told his wife that most men are blinded by "ass, tits, skin color, ultra-sexy and the fact that everyone wants what they have". Mr. Baxter said if you compare the two of them Samantha is extra pretty and dresses sexy and has to be the center of attention. She is a little bit bigger in the booty and the breasts than Rachel. Rachel has the skinnier build and is taller. Rachel has ample breasts and booty but she is not extra-large in either area. Whereas Samantha is light brown skinned Rachel is dark chocolate. Rachel is very conservative in her dressing style. Mr. Baxter says he believes if she could get away with it; Rachel would wear jeans and a baseball cap all the time.

Mr. Baxter said the major difference in them is how they think. Samantha barely can see beyond Samantha White. All Samantha focuses on is her needs and wants. She does not consider how or what she does will affect others. Rachel is all about others and their needs and wants. Mr. Baxter said he would bet his wife $200.00 that when Rachel pulled Julian out of the room it was to talk with him about him? He told Mrs. Baxter that if Julian is honest with you Rachel was checking on him and his state of mind. Mrs. Baxter said she would accept that bet. They were probably talking about material things. Mr. Baxter told Mrs. Baxter that she was wrong. Rachel is not the material things type he told his wife. Besides Rachel is the direct type; if you call her over to our table and ask her what she talked about with Julian she will tell you right now. Mrs. Baxter told her husband that she was going to take him up on his bet. She immediately began waving for Rachel to come to their table.

A short time later Rachel came over and said Hi to Mr. Baxter and sat down with Mrs. Baxter. Rachel told Mrs. Baxter I guess we are now paid employees of the Non-Profit Foundation. They both got a good laugh out of that one. Mrs. Baxter asked Rachel if she discussed the non-profit with Julian when she asked him to leave the room with her. Rachel said no; Julian had brought it up, but she took him out of the room to discuss him as he appeared to be in a daze. She told Mr. and Mrs. Baxter that it appeared to her that Julian was a little bit anxious and troubled about something. We walked and talked a bit about him. He was thinking that he could have done more to keep Samantha White faithful to him. I told him that Samantha White is like some men that want to "taste" every piece of ass that passes them. Samantha just could not see beyond Samantha White and that was why things went down the way they did.

Julian has to stop blaming himself for Samantha. Samantha White is totally to blame. Mr. Baxter told Rachel that she has a huge heart and both Julian and Randle need to find wives like you. Rachel began to blush and stammer. Rachel told Mr. and Mrs. Baxter that Julian, Randall, Pablo and I have been friends since we were kids. Mr. Baxter chimed in; well one member of that posse needs to see how valuable you truly are. They all laughed. A short time later the party ended; and everyone headed out. Julian, Randall, Mr. Baxter and Mrs. Baxter said goodnight to all of the guests. Julian has an early flight, so we are headed back to the hotel to rest. The Baxter family along with Pablo and Rachel headed back to the Hilton Hotel to rest. Julian would be leaving early the next morning for Atlanta by private plane. The family and friends would be headed back on afternoon flights. In the lobby of the Hilton Hotel there was a group hug and then Julian and Randall headed to their room and Mr. and Mrs. Baxter, Pablo and Rachel headed to their respective rooms. Mr. Baxter told Mrs. Baxter she owed him $200 for their bet about Rachel and laughed.

Once they got to their room Randall advised Julian to get his clothes packed and pick out the outfit that he was going to wear. Julian took out a Black three button suit, white long-sleeved button-down collar shirt, black shoes and socks. He got out fresh underwear and a black t-shirt to wear underneath the white shirt. Randall kidded Julian that he should wear a white t-shirt underneath his white shirt. Julian said no he was wearing the black one. Randall suggested he pack every- thing that he did not need out so that he could move quickly in the morning. The Limo would be picking him up at 10am. Randall called the front desk and asked for an 8:30am wakeup call. Randall teased Julian about his prediction of him making it to the NBA. Julian told him he was right on target.

Until Randall and others had started talking about him getting Drafted Julian had never envisioned it. Now here he was about to sign a multi-million-dollar contract. Randall told Julian if he had a problem figuring out what to spend his money on; he had lots of ideas. Julian told him to wait until he was drafted into the NFL and spend his own money.

Randall said he had one question for Julian; what was the meeting between him and Rachel all about? Julian told Randall; Rachel thought that I was looking a little down and she wanted to cheer me up. Randall said you know she has always been positive around all of us; you, me and Pablo. Randall said you have noticed that she has "grown up to be a very attractive lady". Julian said he never paid attention to that. "Whatttttttttttttt?"; said Randall you have got to be kidding me. Granted she is not as big in the areas that Samantha White is; but Rachel looks just like those slim, athletic women on the runway. Just that she has extra breast size and butt size. You may not notice Rachel because you don't pay attention. Besides if Rachel could have her way; she would wear jeans and a baseball cap every day of the year. She has become very beautiful said Randall. She was always attractive but like a rose she has bloomed. Ok said Randall do not take too long to notice before someone steals her from right under your nose. You do know that Rachel adores you Randall told Julian. Even though it killed her inside she was very happy for you and Samantha when you guys hooked up. All you talked about was Samantha White. Some of us noticed how at first it bothered Rachel. She "sucked it up" and came on board because that was "who YOU wanted". You may not recall it now; but I can recall one day at our house when you first developed a crush on Samantha White. You were "Samantha this, Samantha that".

Rachel got up and said she remembered she had to do something at home. She left whenever you would start talking about Samantha for a good while after that. Then she stopped leaving us when you brought Samantha up. She must have decided if that was who you wanted then there was absolutely nothing that she could do about it. "Really"; said Julian. I am 100% correct said Randall. You were and are the only person that does not see how deeply Rachel cares for and about you. That is why she knew you were upset about something and the rest of us did not. She never puts herself first like Samantha White. Rachel cares about all of us but you get top billing with her. Because you cared only about "your queen; Samantha White" you were too busy to notice Rachel. "Really"; said Julian. Yep, said Randall blind to the fact that an "amazing, sensitive, strong, passionate, beautiful, unselfish, loving, caring, smart and ambitious in a good way Lady" loved him. Instead you were "nose wide open" for a selfish, self-centered, spoiled and wannabe diva named Samantha White. Hate to explain the "real facts of life" to you baby brother on this night of all nights. Randall said I bet you if the hotel was on fire and they said they only had room for one person to save and it was the two of you there she would say save YOU and not her. She would rather die than save herself if it was you and her and your lives were on the line. Besides, Randall told Julian Mom will tell you that the main driving force behind your Non-Profit Foundation has been Rachel. She was not ever going to let anything related to you look bad or not work. She spent her money from her other job to ensure that the materials your Non-Profit Foundation sent out were top notch. She purchased supplies before you had sponsors and donations.

Rachel went around and got her friends, former jobs, former co-workers, former classmates and others to donate to your Foundation to get it moving. Ask Mom; Randall told Julian. Rachel was not going to let anything concerning YOU look bad or fail. Now you are on easy street. You owe her more than words Randall told Julian. Seriously; you need to pay attention to her and in some strong way repay her dedication to you and your Foundation. You have millions on top of millions now buy Mom and Dad a home or pay off their mortgage. Give them new cars and do the same for Pablo and Rachel. They deserve it. If it was me that is what I would do. "Really" was all Julian could say. Randall told Julian I have never tried to steer you wrong and I am not steering you wrong now. Before some guy sees the "true value" of Rachel you may want to take the "glaze and friend view off your eyes". She adores you. Randall gave Julian a hug and headed to his part of the two-bedroom suite. Good night baby brother Randall told him and headed to the shower while Julian packed.

Julian shook his head as he recalled Randall's remarks and how Rachel had pulled him out of the room to cheer him up. They had primarily talked about Julian and his concerns. When he had tried to talk about her Rachel had steered the conversation back to about him. She had ended up making him laugh. Then she had brought him back and left him with others. Randall was right she always did that with him. He recalled the look of shock and pain on her face when she had seen him that night looking for Samantha. She could almost feel his pain. Randall was right Rachel cared deeply for him. He had to fix this and at least try to see where the road would lead. He called the front desk and asked them how he could get flowers delivered to a room as he was leaving early in the morning.

The front desk staffer asked Julian which room and the name. He gave them Rachel's room number and name. Julian wanted Rachel to get three dozen red roses and three dozen yellow roses. He told them the delivery needed a card to be attached saying "Miss You and your huge caring heart… See you soon…" Julian is what Julian told them. He paid for the order and hoped he was not too late. Julian showered and crawled into bed wondering how come he never paid attention to Rachel's care and concern for him. He would move to correct all of that right away.

Early the next morning after the wake-up call Julian quickly showered and got dressed. He called the front desk for a bell boy to come and get his luggage. Julian woke up Randall and told him he was leaving for Atlanta. He gave his brother a hug and said he promised to move quickly on the matter they had discussed the night before. Randall told him he had better before it is too late. They both laughed and soon the bellboy was there. The bellboy and Julian headed for the elevator. In the lobby as Julian waited to pay for his room bill he called his parents in their room. Julian let them know that the Limo was there waiting, and he was off to Atlanta. He would call them later. He told his parents to tell Pablo and Rachel that he would be in touch shortly to get the Foundation squared away.

As Julian hung up his phone and headed out to the limo; he could have sworn he heard someone calling his name. He thought he was having hearing issues. The driver and the bellboy put Julian's luggage in the trunk. Julian turned to give the bellboy a $20 tip and out of no-where Rachel appeared. She rushed into Julian's arms and wrapped him up in a bear hug. She was still in her night clothes, night robe and bedroom slippers. Rachel smelled and looked great.

Julian saw Rachel for the first time not as a friend but as a "Beautiful, Smart, Loving, Caring, Lady and Wife. He told her "I missed you so much" and I am sorry that I was so blind. Rachel began to cry and told him that she had always loved him and always would. Julian told the driver we need ten minutes. Julian took Rachel by the hand and walked back to the front desk area. He told Rachel to tell the front desk that his parents would need to check her out. She was leaving now with him. He told her to rush upstairs and get a dress on. Once we get to Atlanta, I will give you my credit card and money to go and buy a dress. Get whatever you need for the Atlanta Hawks Press Conference. Rachel rushed to her room to dress. Julian called his parents and his father answered. Julian told him that he needed him and mom to do him a huge favor. They needed to pack Rachel's stuff and bring it home. She is leaving now with me. She will leave her key at the front desk for you. Let me know if there are any extra expenses. When Rachel opened her door there were six dozen roses in arrangements on the dining room table. Rachel started crying when she read the note. She pulled out one rose from each arrangement and quickly found a dress and also matching shoes. She found clean underwear and rushed into the shower. Soon Rachel was dressed and rushing downstairs. Julian was waiting for her at the front desk. He had used their ATM to get $3000 from his account. He gave her $2500 and kept the rest. He used his credit card to pay for Rachel's room and then gave instructions that his parents would be packing Rachel's stuff. Rachel was smiling as she had the note from the flowers and some of the flowers. They rushed to the limo and piled in. Julian gave the driver $300 for waiting. They were quickly headed to JFK Airport. Julian's phone began ringing; it was his agent Austin LaSalle. Julian said he had some last-minute issues that he had to correct, and he was now on the way to the airport.

Julian told his agent It was all my fault and I will explain later. As long as you are ok Austin said. He was about to call New York's finest. They both started laughing. Austin told Julian I will see you when you get here. Stay safe. Julian told him his lifelong bodyguard was right beside him. Rachel began blushing. Rachel buried her head into his chest and wrapped him up in a bear hug. It felt right. Julian gave her a hug as well. He told her that he was sorry for not paying attention to her before; but he would from now on. She told him not to worry and he had nothing to be sorry about. That was the circumstance then and this is the situation as it stands now. Rachel put her finger to Julian's lips and told him no more apologies. What is in the past stays in the past do you understand? Julian nodded that he understood.

Rachel took her finger from Julian's lips and gave him a long tender kiss. They both became breathless. Julian kept his arms around her as he told her this is the plan; when we get to Atlanta you get a limo and go to Lenox or Phipps and get you several outfits. Hurry back to where-ever we are holding the meetings. Get everything you need to stay there. Get toiletries and everything you need. You will be staying with me. We are going to have to figure some things out on the fly. Once we get there and they tell us what they have in mind. "Know this" Julian told Rachel we are staying together. We will find a home. We will find an office space for the Non-profit Foundation. You get a $150,000 bonus for all the times when you spent your money and went the extra mile for the Foundation and for me. Rachel's response was "really". She told Julian that it was too much. Julian told her that that was just the beginning. Right after we meet with the Atlanta Hawks Management team; we will find a convenient hotel to stay in for a while. Julian told Rachel that later they would find a home of our own to buy.

He told Rachel to remind him that they had to stop at a SunTrust bank to get her a bank card and signing privileges on his accounts. Rachel buried her head in Julian's shoulder again and began crying. Julian held her close and rubbed her back until she stopped crying. He told her she needed to focus. She needed to start thinking about what kind or style house to buy and where. She also needed to start thinking of what style and color Mercedes she wanted. Julian said he did not care if the house had a pool or not but there had to be lots of acreage so that he did not hear his neighbors. It also had to have armed security in the neighborhood. Anything else "your majesty" said Rachel.

The driver rolled down the window between the driver compartment and the passenger compartment; he told Julian that they were ten to twenty minutes away from the airport. He told Julian he had taken a few shortcuts and they should be there soon. Julian told him thanks. The driver rolled the glass up again between the two compartments.

Julian took out his notebook and told Rachel that he needed a few pieces of information from her. What type of jewelry does she like the most; watches, rings, chains? What is her favorite flower? What is her favorite color? What is her ring finger size? What is her wrist size? What is the size of her favorite chain? The rest of the info that he needed could wait he told her. Rachel gave him the info he needed. Julian told her to make sure and let her parents know where she would be. He also urged her to call her regular job and let them know that she would not be coming back. A short time later they were at the airport. Austin LaSalle started laughing when Rachel emerged from the limo. The driver got Julian's bags out and handed them to the staff members of the Private Jet Service firm. They loaded up and soon were on the way to Atlanta.

Julian introduced Rachel as his fiancée. Austin LaSalle gave Rachel one of his business cards in case she had any questions on their matters. Rachel said thanks and put the card in her purse. Paul told Julian and Rachel that once they met with the Hawks Management team; they would have an idea of their schedule and we would be able to plan things. They want to get this done quickly so that they can call a press conference and introduce you right away. We are all going to be staying in the Hilton Hotel right across from the arena. My two associates are on the phone with them now setting up everything. The Hawks are paying for it. We will get you a bigger suite now that we know your fiancée will be with us.

A flight attendant came back and asked Julian, Rachel, Austin and his Associates if they wanted to eat now. Julian asked Rachel what she wanted. She said coffee, creamer, sugar, scrambled eggs and pancakes. Julian said the same for him. Austin said if you have three of those orders; I will have the same. A short time later the attendant was back with coffee, creamers and sugar. A few minutes later she came bearing a tray with food for Rachel, Austin and Julian. They ate up. Austin's two associates only wanted coffee, creamer and sugar. The attendant gave them what they wanted.

After eating Julian, Rachel and Austin decided to relax before their flight hit Atlanta. Austin told Rachel and Julian to get ready for lots of cameras being pointed their way. He also told them that once we meet with the Atlanta Hawks at their office; we will have a better idea of their schedule. We will have a morning session and break for lunch and then we will play things by ear. Austin said it should be a straight -forward negotiation.

The major issues are the signing bonus and the fifth year. We are seeking a $10 to $20 Million dollar signing bonus for you. Austin said he figured at the very least they would get a $10-Million-dollar bonus for Julian. Austin LaSalle, Julian's agent said we are projecting the fifth year pay scale at $12.5 to $18.5 based on the average of the first four years to be $10.3 under the Collective Bargaining Agreement (CBA). Knowing that you faced limits with the salary we went all out to get you as many sponsorship deals as we could with top tier companies. Your big deal with NIKE will fetch $250,000,000.00 for six (6) years. They have also agreed to donate $2.5 million to your foundation. Rachel could not believe her ears as she heard the figures being tossed around by Julian's agent, Austin LaSalle. On top of it the money was all headed towards a man she had known from when they were kids and she had loved all that time. Rachel knew that there was "something special" about Julian all her life. However, when he fell head over heels in love with Samantha White in Middle School; she knew she could not get in the way. She stepped aside and supported him in his quest to win Samantha over. She even befriended Samantha despite the fact that Julian was with her and she wanted Julian beside her holding her hand. Rachel hoped for the best and supported Julian and Samantha. Now here they were side by side; Julian and Rachel. Rachel had never given up on Julian and possibly one day being beside him. Julian was holding tightly on to her hand. Samantha was a fading image in the rearview mirror. Rachel felt that her future with Julian was extremely bright.

Julian turned to Rachel and asked if she was ok? She told Julian this has been the best day of my life and kissed him quickly on the lips. Julian put his arm around her and let her fall back to rest her head on his shoulder. Austin LaSalle looked at Rachel and told Julian to hold on to that woman. She has a calming effect on you and about her. Austin said usually I have never gotten involved in my client's love life because of the world we live in today dynamics can change overnight. But something tells me Julian that you have found a "rare jewel" that I wish all of my clients could find; someone that cares for and about "you" the person. As your agent and friend take care of her. Two working together can achieve more than one alone in 99% of the cases. He said I will leave you two lovebirds alone and check in with my staff in the other area.

Rachel stretched out on the couch and put her head in Julian's lap. Julian took one of the cushions and put it under her head. A minute or two later Rachel was asleep. Julian pressed the buzzer for help. When the flight attendant came to him; he asked her for a blanket or sheet to cover Rachel with. She had fallen fast asleep. The Flight Attendant smiled and commented on how adorable they looked. Julian said take a photo and gave her his Samsung Phone. She snapped several. Julian gave her $40 for her trouble and she hurried away to get him a blanket for Rachel. When she came back; she spread the blanket over Rachel and left them alone. Julian watched Rachel sleep with a smile on his face. He knew she was a hard worker from when they were in middle school.

Rachel was always busy helping someone with their homework and other stuff. Julian had picked up that habit from her. Rachel never asked for repayment. If you had problems with a class or a subject; she would give you the time to help or find someone to help you. Now with his vision clear Julian looked at Rachel and realized what his brother Randall had told him was true. Rachel had that Halle Berry look in a slimmer body type. Julian had to admit he was cockeyed and had looked past Rachel without seeing her as a beautiful Lady. He just saw "Rachel" the girl he, his brother and Pablo had grown up with. Julian closed his eyes and said a short prayer of "Thanks" to God for not letting Rachel get away from him. He already felt good from being close to her and the tingle she gave him when she gave him quick kisses. Julian made a promise to God that he would treasure, protect and highly value Rachel. Julian started smiling. He was going all out to "spoil the heck" out of Rachel for not slapping him awake sooner so that they could have made other memories. But knowing her as he did; she probably said if he was for me; eventually we will get together. If not, life goes on. Rachel was always laid back but fiercely protective of her friends. She had proven that over and over before. Now thought Julian it was time to repay her faith, support and going the extra mile for his young Foundation. First, he would give her an engagement ring as his commitment to her. He would also get her a matching chain and bracelet. Second, he would let her decide where they bought a home. Third he would get her the car of her choice and set up a separate account for her with $1,000,000 in it to do as she pleased with it.

He would also get her a Visa and Amex card in his name with her name on it. He would purchase a life insurance policy worth $30 million with her as the sole beneficiary. That way if anything happened to him she would be taken care of for life.

If her parents had a mortgage it was to be paid off. Each of her parents would get a new car or $45,000.00 each. Fourth, she would have to quit her other job and work only for his Foundation when she was not being wifey. Fifth, she would get flowers every other day for the rest of her life. Whenever he travelled; she would receive gifts. He had indeed found a rare jewel.

On a second thought, forget the engagement ring; they were getting married right away. He was going to buy her a wedding ring. He was not taking any chances of her getting away. Oh no. Julian decided when Rachel wakes up he was going to tell her to start planning her wedding first. Then he would ask her where she wanted to go on her honeymoon.

The Future...

Exactly 52 days later Julian marries Rachel in a lavish wedding ceremony at the Georgia Convention Center. Bishop Todd Rainwater of the Mount Paran Church of God officiated at the ceremony. The wedding was moved to the Georgia Convention Center after a lot of media found out about it and the general public swamped the Foundation web site. Who's Who in sports, business, politics and entertainment was there. There were people helped by Julian's Foundation directly and other people who were helped by Organizations that Julian's Foundation had supported. They remembered where their help had come from. There were also many, many, many fans from Walker High School, University of Miami and the Atlanta Hawks that wanted to attend and see Julian get married. It turned out to be fun event for everyone. There was a huge reception at the Georgia Convention Center complete with cake cutting and the ceremonial "First Dance" to the song "Candle Light and You" by Chante Moore and Keith Washington. Each wedding attendee received a stuffed animal and a t-shirt with a picture of the newlyweds on the front and info on the foundation on the back. One day later the newlyweds headed out for the Bahamas. They went on their honeymoon to the world-famous Atlantis Hotel Resort.

When Julian and Rachel returned from the honeymoon the two along with Randall, Pablo and Mrs. Baxter coordinated a massive neighborhood block party. They went five times the size of the last one. They ordered lots of food, blocked off the road and had play- rooms, jump rooms, splash pools, slides and other games for the children. Tables and chairs were rented and placed in the road along with umbrellas and tents for shade. There were three times as many portable toilets. A DJ was hired for the event. The party started at 9am on Saturday and lasted into Sunday morning. Free T-shirts in an assortment of colors and styles were given to the attendees. Stuffed animals were given to the children. Julian autographs everything the attendees brought to the event.

Julian receives a $15 million dollar signing bonus from the Hawks. He signs with the Air Jordan brand at NIKE and gets a $250-Million-dollar contract for 6 years. Nike gives him a $12 million dollar signing bonus. He signs on with Mercedes Benz, Pepsi-Cola, SunTrust Bank, Domino's Pizza, National Car Rental, Rolex Watches and Delta Air Lines. His agent gets him top dollar from his sponsors as he already has name and brand recognition. His recognition is high all over the country and even in Brazil, China, Russia, The Caribbean and Canada. The Brink's truck has to carry all the money Julian begins to make in the NBA. Once he signs with the Atlanta Hawks and his sponsors and the initial bonus checks arrive. Rachel and Mrs. Baxter meet with various neighbors and community groups to find the main needs for kids, families and the neighborhood.

The Recreation Center near them that houses the Boys and Girls club has fallen on hard times. Julian asks his mother to find the contractor that supplied the portable toilets to get the name of a good builder. Julian and his mother ask for the name of a good builder to rebuild the Boys and Girls Club from the ground up. It was decided it would be cheaper in the long run to build a new complex. Once the costs are figured out. In order to modernize the building, add more courts, swimming pools indoor and outside, updated parking area, updated tennis courts and ball field it would cost $7 Million for the facilities and $1.1 million for the additional land. Julian has his mother and Rachel get a cashier's check for the money and also give the Boys & Girls club an additional $150,000.00 for operational costs and camps while the new facilities are being built.

Julian sets up a scholarship fund Program. He knows full well that High School and College are expensive these days. Scholarships are awarded to deserving students in the neighborhood to high school and college. Several families were going through extreme financial hardship and they received varying "gifts" from the foundation in amounts ranging from $5,000 to $20,000. The recipients are asked to pay it back by being of assistance to others in the community and the neighborhood. Several churches in the area were given donations for their youth and community programs. There were people that needed cars as their vehicles were constantly dying. They received top notch used vehicles from the Marietta Mercedes Benz Dealership. They also received the funds to pay for their auto insurance for six months. Each vehicle was given a 24-month warranty Free of Charge.

Julian donates $2 Million to his High school and told them to let him know what else they needed. The baseball team needed new equipment and uniforms. NIKE took care of the uniforms and equipment. The baseball team received a $150,000 check as did the men's and women's basketball teams.

Rachel and Pablo are hired by the Foundation to raise money and to find out the needs and wants of the community. Two more staff members are hired at the Foundation. The Foundation is moved to its own building. It is built from the ground up with the latest security and computer systems. Rachel, Pablo and Mrs. Baxter take the lead in designing the new building. Rachel, Pablo and Mrs. Baxter and the other staff members are charged with ensuring that the Foundation continues to grow and also has a positive impact on the community and neighborhood. They work directly with Mrs. Baxter. She left the bank to become Co-Executive Director with Rachel and spearhead the Foundation. All of the companies that Julian becomes a spokesman for donate to the Foundation. They also referred friends to the Foundation. Julian said; "to whom much is given much more is expected".

Julian paid off his parent's home mortgage and gave them new Mercedes cars along with Rachel and Pablo. His parents do not want a new home so Julian gave them $1 Million dollars. Julian gave Pablo $750,000.00 to purchase his own home. Rachel's parents had their mortgage paid off and were given new cars plus $1 Million dollars. Randall was drafted by the Miami Dolphins football team so he could afford his own car.

Randall still received a $1,000,000 check from Julian for always being there for him. Brian was drafted by the Miami Heat but still received a $500,000.00 check for being a friend. Julian kept the Dodge Charger Silver Bullet car.

Julian donated $1 million to the University of Miami. He also gave $150,000 each to the women's programs in Atlanta and Miami for abused women or women that are single parents.

Julian goes on to be named Rookie of the year in the NBA posting a 26-point, 11 rebound and 8 assist average. He also had explosions of 40, 45 and 58 points in a game. He sets up a section for all Atlanta Hawks home games where kids from shelters, low income and others can come to a game and have good seats FREE. He pays for their transport to and from the game, tickets and food.

Julian and Rachel receive a ton of awards for their charity and also the work of the Foundation. To surprise her Julian has Rachel's full name written in the sky over Atlanta with the phrase "I will always Love and Treasure you...Forever yours...Julian Baxter". All the TV and Radio stations talk about it. Someone films the writing in the sky; and it goes viral on social media. Their Love Story becomes a best-selling book.

...The End...

Mystery Lady...
My Muse...
My Inspiration...

Publishing Division of Black Eagle Group

Peter Giant Bowleg

Author

Books on amazon.com by Peter Giant Bowleg include:

- Black Eagle – Stand [Action/Adventure]
- "What are your Dreams...?" (I See Greatness In YOU) [Advice]
- Run To The Light [Poetry & Short Stories to Inspire]

Coming Soon...

- Most Valuable Player [Overcoming the odds in Life...story]
- Miss IT [Children's story about a dog called Miss IT]
- Judgement Day for SAVAGES [Action/Adventure]
- BlackLand [A New Beginning]
- The State of Black America [Perspective]
- Fade to Black [A Love Story]
- Black Eagle – Shadow Warriors [Action/Adventure]
- Believe – All Things Are Possible [Inspirational]
- Roosevelt the Rottweiler [Children's story]
- My Angel - [A Love Story]

"...MAKE YOUR HATERS YOUR MOTIVATORS..."

"...Most Valuable Player..."

(I See GREATNESS In YOU...)

Soundtrack

"It's Time..." - The Winans & Teddy Riley...
"Optimistic" - Sounds of Blackness...
"Too Legit to Quit" - MC Hammer...
"Adventure" - Coldplay...
"I've Got The Power" - Snap...
"I'm Still Waiting" - Jodeci...
"U and I" - Jodeci...
"When will I see you smile" - Bell, Biv, Devoe...
"There you go" - Johnny Gill...
"Say Yes" - Floetry...
"Lately" - Tyrese...
"Candle Lights and you" - Chante Moore & Keith Washington...
"Whatever it takes" - Anita Baker...
"Lose Control" - Silk...
"Can I borrow you" - Eric Roberson...
"Seven Days" - Mary J featuring George ....
"No ordinary Love" - Sade...
"Love Calls" - Kem...
"Good Life" - Anita Baker...
"Your Smile" - Rene & Angela...
"Never too busy" - Kenny Lattimore...
"I cant stop loving you" - Kem...
"The Secret Garden" - Quincy Jones...

"...Most Valuable Player..."

(I See GREATNESS In YOU...)

Soundtrack

"Angel" - Anita Baker...
"Cherish the day" - Sade...
"Love saw it" - Karyn White & Babyface...
"You put a move on my heart" - Tamia...
"Baby come to me" - Regina Bell...
"Alone with You..." - Tevin Campbell...
"Always..." - Pebbles...
"I'll Give You Everything..." - After 7...
"Get Up..." - Mary Mary...
"Go Get IT..." - Mary Mary...
"Lately" - Anita Baker...

Reference

- Wikipedia
- Google.com
- ESPN Network
- NCAA.com
- NBA.com
- Miami Heat Team
- Atlanta Hawks Team
- Dick's Sporting Store – Staff Members Info
- FedEx Office – Windy Hill & Perimeter Locations
- Atlanta Hawks
- NBA Corporate Office, New York
- University of Miami
- University of Georgia
- Kennesaw State University
- Georgia Tech
- A Mystery Lady

(I See GREATNESS In YOU...)

Director of Graphics

Mr. Scot Mmobuosi
www.scotdesigns.com

Phone: [914]-714-0027
Email: scot@scotdesigns.com

Scot Banye Mmobuosi is a visual and graphic artist as well as a web designer. His background in Mathematics and Architecture have helped in enhancing is artistic talent by incorporating precision and details. His ability to draw exceptionally has enabled him work for animation companies, writers and graphic novelists. In fact he is involved as the artist of the graphic novel series called "The Tales of Conquest" (http://www.talesofconquest.com) which would be out soon. Scot also has tremendous computer graphic skills and uses this to create images and other visuals, no matter how complex. He feels, anything that can be imagined can be created.

In addition to these, Scot also builds website, both corporate and personal. He believes his background in Mathematics has a big influence in this.

For more information on Scot's works, please visiting his portfolio website at http://www.scotdesigns.com and feel free to contact him.

Scot B. Mmobuosi
www.scotdesigns.com

"...Most Valuable Player..."

(I See GREATNESS In YOU...)

The Message...

Never, Ever Give Up On Your Dreams...

Whenever you are trying to do something, achieve something or make a difference there will be "haters and obstacles". You can count on it. There will be self-appointed critics that have "done nothing" with their lives and have no dreams or goals. Never panic. Never get distracted.

Keep moving forward...

There will be those that promise and swear to be there to help make your program or project a reality. Be ready for disappointment and Keep moving forward...

There will be people that you really care about who will let you down...

Keep moving forward...

There will be issues with the program, project and finances...

Keep moving forward...

In the end; the satisfaction of completing your project, program, record or book despite the lack of support will energize you for the rest of your life...

Keep moving forward...

(I See GREATNESS In YOU...)

Peter Giant Bowleg

Author

Dreamer, Encourager, Loner, the smiling Man in Black, Usher at Mount Paran Church of God, Son, Brother, Father, Friend, Cousin, Nephew, Relative and Believer are some of the Ways he is known. Born in the Bahamas he was Educated in the USA. He is the son of Theresa Fairweather of Florida and the Bahamas Islands. One of seven children his Brothers and Sisters are Andrew, Paulette, Judy, Ethan, Trevor and BJ. He has two sons – Tavares and Valentino Bowleg living in the Bahamas. His new book "...What Are Your Dreams...?" are his thoughts and ideas of bringing a change to the way Black and Minority Young People and adults see themselves. He believes change the picture in the mirror and Change the person's life and legacy. He has spent Over 30 years in Corporate America. He has worked at Citibank, Shell, Texaco, United Waste, Carnival Cruise Lines, Lou Bachrodt Chevrolet and others. He has started Publishing and Consulting firm in Atlanta Georgia called Black Eagle Group. It was created to publish his books, provide Consulting Services and coordinate the Program he has created under the book – What are your dreams. He gives a "third eye Consulting view of Business and Marketing" for Companies and individuals.

He has written four other books – "Run To The Light" A book of poetry and short stories designed to uplift. "What are your Dreams?" A book designed to help a person young or old find their path and passion. "Black Eagle – STAND and Judgement Day for SAVAGES". These are two action books that he created. All of the books are on amazon.com under his full name Peter Giant Bowleg. He has a passion for God, Family, Life, Fellow Man, Woman and Child. Be Blessed...

"...LISTEN...ENCOURAGE...INSPIRE...UPLIFT..."

Email: blackeagleent@yahoo.com
Email: wayd19@yahoo.com
www.blackeaglenation.net
www.wetalknow.net

"...Make your haters your Motivators...
Never Give IN, Never Ever Give UP.
The BEST Revenge is to life the GOOD LIFE..."
- Julian "JB" Baxter – NBA Star
The Mystery Dunker

"...Act like a Success...
Think like a Success..."

Julian Baxter could play basketball well. For some reason he played great in practice but when the games began; he would play poorly. Julian worked hard, practiced and practiced. He was the last man off the bench. Then he had a "life-changing experience". He becomes a "NEW MAN". He becomes the "Most Valuable Player".

"...Hidden inside anyone can be a Champion
waiting for the opportunity to shine
and become... **The MVP**..."